Taking Care of Terrific

Also by Lois Lowry

A Summer to Die
Find a Stranger, Say Goodbye
Anastasia Krupnik
Autumn Street
Anastasia Again!
Anastasia at Your Service

Taking Care of Terrific

LOIS LOWRY

Houghton Mifflin Company   Boston

Library of Congress Cataloging in Publication Data

Lowry, Lois.
  Taking care of Terrific.

  Summary: Taking her overprotected young charge to
the public park to broaden his horizons, fourteen-year-
old baby sitter Enid enjoys unexpected friendships with
a black saxophonist and a bag lady until she is charged
with kidnapping.
  [1. Baby sitters—Fiction. 2. Parks—Fiction.
3. Boston (Mass.)—Fiction] I. Title.
PZ7.L9673Tak 1983   [Fic]   82-23331
ISBN 0-395-34070-5

Printed in the United States of America

HAD 10 9 8 7

For Erik and Richard

Keep a green tree in your heart and perhaps the singing bird will come.

— Chinese proverb

Chapter 1

I threw down the book I'd been trying to read, stared out of my bedroom window for a while at the tops of the trees, sighed, and picked up my sketch pad. I doodled a few designs: leaves and stems curling around each other, intertwined. Carefully I colored in the leaves with a green marking pen, leaving some white spots for highlights, so that they looked glossy and radiant.

Maybe, I thought glumly, I'd feel better if someone sprinkled me with fertilizer. Plants do.

Once I bought a dumb little jade plant at a street fair. It really needed somebody; it looked crummy and neglected, like an orphan who's never been taken to the zoo. I gave it to my mother on her birthday, and she took over with her little tweezers and tweakers and her bottles of plant food, talking to it: "There, now. This will make you perk up," and eureka, it perked up. Grew. Flourished.

Probably my mother talked like that to me

when I was little. She hasn't for a long time, though. My parents chose the Carstairs School because in the catalogue it said, "We encourage independence." (It also said, "We charge fifty-two hundred dollars a year tuition for day students, plus lab fees and books, and our graduates get into the best Ivy League college"; but the thing that hooked my parents was the "We encourage independence.")

Murmuring "There now, this will perk you up" to a fourteen-year-old girl probably does not encourage independence. So that is why my mother says that only to small droopy plants suffering from aphids or root rot. To me, when I look, feel, and am droopy, discouraged, depressed, and practically about to throw myself out of my bedroom window because nothing in my life seems to go the way I want it to, my mother says, "Enid, for heaven's sake, you have to learn to solve your own problems. And it might be a start if you would do something about your *hair*."

Sometimes I wish I were a philodendron.

If I were a philodendron, I would not be sitting here, a prisoner in my own bedroom, thinking about what happened this summer, scared stiff and super miserable.

It was the best summer of my life. I found

some new friends. They were friends who *needed* me. They were wilted. I tried to encourage them to bloom, just the way my mother coaxes her begonias into blossoming. And it worked. I saw it work. We put the whole thing together so that on one night — just last week, a night I'll never forget no matter what happens, and even if I never see most of those friends again — on that night we were all together, and a thin slice of moon was shining; there was music playing, and the green was all around us so green that you could feel it down inside your soul, and everybody's life was changed. At least for an hour. Maybe that is all you ever get in this world, one hour like that.

Then, of course, came the horrible rest of it: police, some on shiny-hooved horses, others in cars with blue lights flashing; newspaper people yelling questions that had no answers; a TV guy with a camera balanced on his shoulder. Bright lights and bright lights and bright lights; handcuffs and shoving and a loudspeaker. Finally, in the police station, my parents. My mother actually had no make-up on; they'd gotten her out of bed. Very few people have ever seen my mother with no make-up. And until that night, I doubt if *anyone* had ever seen my mother cry.

And now I've been in my bedroom for a week:

my bedroom with the yellow bedspread that I once thought made me feel cheerful all the time. It doesn't anymore.

Downstairs, people have been coming and going for a week. Conferences have been held in my father's study. My father is a lawyer, and he is representing me even though he hasn't handled a criminal case in years. From my window I can see the taxis and the cars come, and I can see the people come up the front steps of our house. Policemen in uniform. Lawyers, one of them a man with a face like a frozen leather glove. Wilma Sandroff, the world-famous child psychologist, hotshot expert on getting in touch with your feelings, which is a lot of crap because Wilma Sandroff hasn't been in touch with her own feelings in about forty-nine years, and I happen to know that her own three children hate her guts. And that one of them, her oldest, is at this very moment sitting in his own bedroom three blocks away.

Well, I don't want to think about him now.

They are all downstairs negotiating. What they are negotiating is what is going to happen to me.

If I have to go to jail, I wonder if they will let me keep a little green plant in my cell.

Chapter 2

*J*ust to put things into the right perspective: I changed my name *first*. *Before* the kidnapping — and all the other crimes they're accusing me of.

So it was not that I was using an alias, the way the newspapers said.

It was this way. I have always hated my name: Enid Irene Crowley. Now really. It would be a terrible name even for an old woman; for a fourteen-year-old girl it was unbearable.

Maybe you have never noticed, but the most hideous adjectives end in the letter *d*. Pick up any one of Stephen King's horror novels and open to any page; you'll find them: horrid, putrid, sordid, acrid, viscid, squalid. And the very worst: *fetid*. Probably you don't even know what "fetid" means; it isn't a word you hear people use very often. But if you read a lot, the way I do, especially horror books, you come across that word, usually describing the breath of creatures who have returned from the grave and are covered with green slime. They all have fetid breath.

Enid isn't a repulsive adjective, as far as I know. But it sounds as if it should be. I find myself making up sentences with the word "enid" in them. Like: "She had been trapped in the crypt for seventeen days; her fingernails had begun to rot, she was suffering from gangrene of the toes, and her once-lustrous blond hair had become limp and enid, with moss growing in it."

You can see why I decided to change my name.

Of course I didn't do it legally. Since my father is a lawyer, I suppose he would know how. But I couldn't ask my father to do that. It was his great-aunt whom I was named for: the very rich one. I think they hoped that she would leave her money to me. She didn't, of course. She left it all to a residential home for seafaring men; no one could figure out why, and they tried to contest the will. But apparently she was of very sound mind when she wrote it, and all the money went to the seafaring men, whoever they are. I hope they bought a whole assortment of video games and that they have seafood dinners sent in from Pier 4 every night.

I figure my great- aunt Enid probably had a love affair with a sea captain once. Good for her.

During the whole time I knew her, she lived all alone in a house on Beacon Hill, with velvet draperies pulled tightly closed so that it was always dark. She read all the novels of Henry James, one after another; and when she finished the last one, she began at the beginning again. She died with *The Portrait of a Lady* open in her hands at page 143.

I sure *hope* she had a love affair with a sea captain once. If all you ever get out of life is the novels of Henry James, it hardly seems worthwhile putting in your eighty-three years.

I myself have always intended to get a great deal more than that out of life. But I thought that with a name like Enid, my chances weren't too good.

So — informally — I began to call myself Cynthia as soon as school ended in June. When I made an appointment to have my hair trimmed at Antone's on Newbury Street, I made the appointment in the name of Cynthia Crowley. When I was stopped by a man on Berkeley Street one day and asked to sign a petition denouncing transvestites, I signed the petition as Cynthia Crowley, even though I wasn't exactly sure what transvestites were. And when I enrolled in the morning art classes at the Museum of Fine Arts,

I enrolled as Cynthia Crowley. I decided that I would spend the summer meeting new people and maybe becoming something of a new person myself.

I decided that my new life was going to have elements of romance, intrigue, danger, and pathos in it. I thought of it as a menu from which I could order two from Column A and one from Column B.

I was supposed to spend my spare time making sketches for my art class. I decided to do that in my very favorite green place, the Public Garden, which is just two blocks from my house. I decided that in the Public Garden, where I would be Cynthia, I could also find romance, intrigue, danger, and pathos.

If that sounds foolish to you, it only means that you don't know Boston.

Chapter 3

*M*y mother is a radiologist. She can do stuff like aim a billion volts of lethal rays at a microscopic mole on somebody's big toe. So you would think she'd be very perceptive, right? You'd think she'd be able to see what's going on around her all the time, right?

Wrong.

She *hires* people to keep track of things. At work, she hires people who tell her what patients she has to see that day, what meetings she has to go to, maybe even what day of the week it is.

At home, she has Mrs. Kolodny. My mother hired Mrs. Kolodny years ago — fourteen, to be exact — when I was born. Mrs. Kolodny lives in our house, and she is supposed to keep track of things here; she is supposed to keep track of me. Most of the time it is the other way around. Mrs. Kolodny is one of the flakiest people I have ever met. In fourteen years, my mother has never noticed this.

Mrs. Kolodny watches soap operas from one to three every afternoon, sitting on a plastic drop-cloth that she puts over a chair in the study so that she won't wrinkle the chair.

In the morning she watches the Donahue show. Sometimes she tells me, with great satisfaction, "Donahue had more of those preverts on today. People called in from all over and condemned them."

"Preverts," to Mrs. Kolodny, means gay people, divorced people, people with open marriages, people who belong to any religion she hasn't heard of, and one time a woman who had a pet ocelot. She really hates it when Donahue has a politician or an environmentalist on his show.

When she's not watching TV, Mrs. Kolodny reads. Mostly she reads gothic romances. The heroines are always named things like Serena or Valerie, and they are always seduced by sinister men whom they encounter on cliffs during thunderstorms. It always surprises Mrs. Kolodny when they are seduced.

"Listen to this, Enid," she said to me one morning, moving her finger under a line of print in a book. " 'We mustn't, Jonathan,' whispered

Catherina as he began roughly to remove her rain-spattered gown. 'Please, Jonathan. I am promised to Lord Farquhar! We mustn't!' "

"Yeah," I said.

"She meant it, too," said Mrs. Kolodny. "She'd been promised to that lord since she was twelve!"

"Yeah," I said.

"And then on the very next page," Mrs. Kolodny said angrily, "she forgot all her very principles. How can someone forget all her principles in *one page?*"

"Beats me," I said.

Mrs. Kolodny sighed, marked her place in the book, and went off to run the vacuum cleaner for a few minutes.

When she isn't watching TV or reading, Mrs. Kolodny cleans. She does all her cleaning during commercials or between chapters.

After a war approximately the size of World War II, she stopped cleaning my bedroom. I started that war myself, after Mrs. Kolodny had vacuumed up an entire science experiment that was laid out on my desk. She said it was rotten bananas and cookie crumbs. I said it was genetic research on fruit flies.

Mom tried to remain neutral because she did

sort of like the idea of my doing scientific research, although she sympathized with Mrs. Kolodny on hygienic grounds.

Dad tried to stay out of it altogether, but Mrs. Kolodny told him that the vacuum cleaner needed eighty-five dollars' worth of repairs because the rotten banana had fouled up its insides. Then Dad said that was it, that was absolutely *it*, and she was not to clean my room anymore, ever.

My room is on the top floor of our house on Marlborough Street. The fifth. And Mrs. Kolodny has what my mom says is phlebitis, but Mrs. Kolodny calls it housemaid's knee, and she always hated going up to the fifth floor.

We get along okay now that she doesn't clean my room anymore. Sometimes I give her backrubs. And we talk about books. There's not much to say about gothic romances, but every now and then she surprises me and reads something intellectual, like *Moby Dick*. She got fascinated with *Moby Dick*, which she borrowed from me when I had to read it for school, and for a long time we talked about whaling and how neat it would be to go out on a whaling ship. I think, though, that she envisioned it stopping in the Virgin Islands now and then, like a cruise ship, and thought she could do lots of duty-free shopping. It seemed like a good way of life to her, harpooning whales for a few days, melting down blubber, and then sipping a piña colada and taking a swim at St. Croix. There would be no preverts around. I think she had the idea that Gregory Peck would be along.

The problem with most people's lives is that they have lost the capacity to believe that Gregory Peck would be along.

"Enid," said Mrs. Kolodny one morning as I came in from my art class, "some woman called. She wants you to babysit."

"Okay. Who was it? When does she want me?"

Mrs. Kolodny's face froze into her glazed expression. One of the things I know about Mrs. Kolodny, that my mother doesn't know, is that she can't remember things. Certain things fall out of her brain like water falling through a sieve. When that happens, she gets this expression on her face; her eyes glaze as if someone has frosted her onto the top of a cake and she will be like that, staring into space, forever. I know how to deal with it, though.

"Think back," I said. "The phone rang. It was

a woman, and she asked for me, and I wasn't home. What did she say?"

The glazed frosting began to melt on her face, and she thought. "She said she knew your mother from the Civil Club."

"There isn't any Civil Club, Mrs. Kolodny. My mother belongs to the Civic Association and the Civil Liberties Union. It must have been one of those."

The glazed look again. She was drawing a blank.

"Well," I told her, "that part doesn't matter. Think back. Can you remember her name?"

She thought some more. "I wrote it down," she said finally.

"Which phone?"

She brightened. "Kitchen. I was starting to do the laundry and reading *Passion at Penzance*. I answered the phone in the kitchen."

The washing machine was thumping away in the kitchen. The paperback copy of *Passion at Penzance* had a coupon for twenty-five cents off a pound of Maxwell House coffee stuck in it as a bookmark and was lying on the table. Standing on top of the dryer, next to the washing machine, was a large box of instant mashed potatoes. I had a horrible feeling about that, but I let it pass for a moment. On the pad of paper by the phone was written, in Mrs. Kolodny's tiny, scrunched handwriting: "Mz Cameron, babysit." Under that was a telephone number.

"Mrs. Kolodny," I said, before I dialed Ms. Cameron's number, "why are the instant mashed potatoes on top of the dryer?"

She looked. "Omigod," she said.

"You didn't."

"Omigod. I had them out to thicken the chowder. And the box is the same size —"

"As the detergent box, right?"

"Omigod."

"You want to look or shall I?"

She just groaned. I looked. It wasn't too bad. Lumpy, but not disastrous. I found the box of Tide, put the instant potatoes back in the cupboard, and told Mrs. Kolodny, "Just let it run. Then do the clothes again with the Tide. It's not the end of the world." I rubbed her back for a minute because she looked so humiliated, and a backrub is always good for humiliation.

Ms. Cameron answered the phone on the second ring, and I could picture her from her voice. Young. Tall. Cheekbones. The sort of voice that has gone to all the best schools and knows which syllables to pronounce which way. She was the

15

kind of person who would wear only unobtrusive make-up, who would eat yogurt, listen to chamber music, ride a bike, jog, and save whales. But her bike would be a four-hundred-dollar Peugeot, and she would have the yogurt delivered from DeLuca's, along with cases of the right wine. She would go to antinuclear demonstrations wearing designer jeans and monogrammed sweaters from Land's End.

Funny how you can tell all of that from a voice.

She would no doubt have a rosy-cheeked baby with a biblical name, brought up on breast milk and natural foods. She would have read books about parenting. The baby would ride around in an expensive carrier on her back.

I made arrangements to take her kid — naturally there was only one; she would be into zero population growth — to the Public Garden that afternoon after his nap. Ms. Cameron would be taking her harpsichord lesson then.

I had planned to go to the Public Garden that afternoon anyway, to start my new life, and I liked the idea of having a kid with me. I like to babysit. It's a good feeling to have somebody need you, and nobody needs you more than a little kid who has wet diapers or scraped knees and who looks at you and cries and holds up his arms.

"Mrs. Kolodny," I said, "I'll watch *As the World Turns* with you after lunch, but then I'm going to babysit."

She got her glazed look again. "Lunch," she said. "Omigod."

"What's the problem with lunch? There's that chowder on the stove." But as soon as I said it, I knew. "Mrs. Kolodny. You *didn't*."

But she had. It's absolutely astounding that in fourteen years my mother has never realized that Mrs. Kolodny is such a space cadet. What an enormous secret to keep.

She and I dumped the chowder thickened with Tide down the garbage disposal. Then we opened a can of Chunky soup and shared it for lunch.

Chapter 4

*J*oshua Warwick Cameron IV. I knew it.

I liked him, though. He had thick blond hair cut like Buster Brown, corduroy overalls right out of a *New Yorker* ad, and he looked very suspicious of me when his mother introduced us.

I liked it that he looked suspicious. Even though his mother had obviously gone through Charm School with straight A's, old Joshua Warwick Cameron IV, age four, was still half asleep and not too thrilled that his mom was urging him to shake hands with someone named Enid Crowley.

"Ms. Cameron," I said, giving old Joshua time to wake up and assess the situation, "do you know my mother very well?"

"No," she said. "I met her at a meeting, and when she mentioned that she had a teenage daughter, I just happened to ask if you'd be interested in babysitting, afternoons. Why?"

"Well, I guess she didn't have a chance to tell

you that I really prefer to be called by my middle name, Cynthia. It gets kind of complicated, because my parents like to call me Enid. So if you call me up or anything, it's easier to ask for Enid. But I really like Cynthia better."

"Oh. I see. Yes, I can understand that. My own parents still call me Elizabeth, although everyone else has called me Betsy for years. Joshua, sweetie, this is Cynthia. She's going to take you to the Public Garden."

Joshua yawned. He looked at me carefully, now that his eyes were wide open, and finally he nodded.

"Okay," he said. "I'll go get my sweater."

Ms. Cameron began giving me instructions. Don't let him pat dogs because you never know about strange dogs.

Okay.

Make him keep his sweater on because she doesn't want him to catch cold; he is very prone to ear infections.

Okay.

No candy or other sweets. She is very careful about sweets because she doesn't want him to get cavities.

Okay.

Explain to him about not picking the flowers in

the Public Garden because it is against the rules, although certainly she wants him to enjoy *looking* at the flowers.

Okay.

Watch him so that he doesn't fall into the pond, but don't make him feel *fearful* about the pond.

Okay.

And especially don't let him talk to any strangers because, well, you know the sorts of people who might be hanging around the Public Garden; you just never can tell.

Actually, there are all sorts of interesting people hanging around the Public Garden. But from the way she said it with a kind of knowing look, a just-between-us-adults sort of attitude, I could tell that she meant: don't let him talk to what Mrs. Kolodny would call preverts, people who would kidnap old Joshua for weird sexual reasons.

I said okay.

He came trotting back down the hall, dragging a little Irish sweater and carrying a stuffed bear. His mother buttoned him into the sweater and tried very pleasantly to take away the bear.

He held on tightly. "Bearable wants to go along," he said.

"Sweetie," said his mother, trying the old child

psychology, "Bearable has a cold, I think. I heard him coughing this morning. He really should stay home in bed."

"No," said Joshua, outpsychologizing her. "I gave him penicillin."

"It's all right," I told her. "I don't mind. I'll keep an eye on Bearable, too."

So off we went, me and Joshua Warwick Cameron IV, and Bearable staring glassy-eyed at the brick sidewalk from under his master's arm, down West Cedar Street to Chestnut, and down Chestnut to Charles, on our way to the Public Garden.

On our way, we stopped and patted a large Airedale tied to a post in front of the bookstore, thereby breaking rule one.

We took off his sweater because it really was pretty warm, breaking rule two.

And we stopped at DeLuca's, where I bought some Life Savers, and we each ate one, breaking rule three.

All that was before we even *got* to the Garden.

The other thing we did, which was not really breaking a rule because his mother hadn't told us not to, was old Joshua's idea, and it made me realize that he and I were going to get along just fine. We changed his name.

As we stood at the corner of Beacon and Charles, waiting for the light, I said, "Watch for it to turn green, Joshua."

"Don't call me that," he said firmly. Then he added politely, "Please."

I asked him if he would like me to call him Josh.

"No," he said thoughtfully, trotting beside me as we crossed the street. "I want you to call me Tom."

"Tom Mix? Or Uncle Tom?" I asked, wondering if he knew about old cowboy movies or Harriet Beecher Stowe.

"Nope," he said. "Tom Terrific."

So the kid was allowed to watch cartoons. I remembered Tom Terrific; he had that Wonder Dog, Manfred. Mrs. Kolodny and I used to watch them together, back when I was just a little kid.

At the entrance to the Public Garden, we had a small name-changing ceremony, my little four-year-old buddy and I. We shook hands solemnly after he shifted Bearable to his other arm, then we each popped another Life Saver — he liked the green ones best — into our mouths. We entered the Garden holding hands. Cynthia, and Tom Terrific. Those other people, Enid Crowley and Joshua Warwick Cameron IV, whoever they were, got left behind, at least for the afternoon.

It looked as if it might be a pretty good summer.

Chapter 5

I have this theory that it's very important to know your turf well. Up until then, my main turf had been my bedroom, and I know my bedroom very, very well. I know my room as well as I know my parents, or Mrs. Kolodny, or Emily and Trina, my best friends from school.

I know that my bed once belonged to my grandmother, who died when I was little, probably right around the time I was wearing corrective shoes and wishing I had a Wonder Dog named Manfred. I remember that I had a Youth Bed, with a plastic covering over the mattress in case I might still wet at night. Then all of a sudden I had this big mahogany fourposter that had been my grandmother's, because my grandmother had died. I suspect that she died in the very same bed, but I have never gotten my mother to admit it.

"Enid," says my mother when I ask her exactly *where* my grandmother died, "she died at home, very peacefully." (That means *bed*, right? Would you die peacefully in the shower?)

"Enid," says my mother, "the exact location is not at all important." (I wonder if she says that to her patients as she aims her million-volt X-ray machines at them. "The exact location is not at all important, tra-la. Head, stomach, knee, somewhere around there; relax.")

I like to think that my grandmother died in her — my — bed. The thought doesn't gross me out. It gives me a sense of history.

"Tom Terrific," I said to Joshua Cameron, "this is going to be our turf. The Public Garden. So we have to get to know it really well."

Tom Terrific looked at me with that frowned-up sort of face that four-year-olds get when they don't know what you're talking about.

"Why do we have to do that?" he asked.

I thought for a minute. I wanted to tell him all about green places: how everyone needs a green place in his life, a place where you can be whatever you want to be, a place where you feel alive and ageless. If you are fourteen, like me (*adolescent*, Famous Psychologist Wilma Sandroff says; God, how I hate that word *adolescent*), it doesn't matter in your green place. You can be three, or forty, or eighty — whatever you want to be. And if you are four, like Joshua Warwick Cameron IV (what would Wilma Sandroff call four? Early Childhood? How I hate Wilma Sandroff), you wouldn't have to be four anymore. You could be a hundred and nine, if you chose, in your green place. You could be Tom Terrific.

But I realized he would be a little confused by all of that.

He pulled at my sleeve. "Why is this our turf?" he asked. "Why do we have to get to know it really well?"

I thought of an answer he might understand. "Because," I said, "it's where we escape from the enemy."

Tom Terrific was mulling over that bit of information (and smiling; he understood about the need to escape from the enemy) when suddenly he was whomped on the head. Not by a weapon. Not by a club or a blackjack or anything. But by a huge, soft, black purse. The woman who was carrying it hadn't meant to hit him. It was just that he was so short. As she walked past, her fat pocketbook knocked the top of his blond head and almost wiped him out. Some babysitter I was turning out to be; it would be tough to explain, bringing him home with a concussion.

"Hey!" I said to the woman who had hit him. She turned, startled, and looked back at her victim, who was rubbing the top of his head and deciding whether or not to cry.

"Well," she muttered, "don't stand in the middle of the path, then." She turned and walked on. Hobbled, really. She wasn't too great at walking, maybe because her shoes were both untied, so that she was tripping herself, and her ankles looked swollen. Also, her gray hair was in her eyes, so she could barely see where she was going. And her long black coat (this was July. Hot. I had already taken Tom Terrific's sweater off) flapped around her like a giant bat.

"Is that the enemy?" Tom asked. I could see that he was intrigued by the idea of enemies. And his head was okay. Her purse was overstuffed and probably just as soft as Bearable, who was still under Tom's arm.

"No. It's just a bag lady."

"What's a bag lady?"

Boy, did Tom Terrific have a lot to learn. Probably his mother had taught him every nursery rhyme that Mother Goose ever dreamed up, and probably he knew the words to the Apostles' Creed and also the seven warning signals of cancer. But no one had ever told him about bag ladies.

"Well, first of all," I told him, "they're ladies. You know what ladies are."

"Yep."

"And usually they're kind of old."

"The one who whomped me on the head was old."

"And they're poor," I said.

Tom Terrific thought about that for a moment. "What's 'poor'?" he asked.

What's "poor"? Tough to explain that one to a kid who lives in a huge house on one of Boston's most exclusive streets and whose Teddy bear has a Steiff label.

"They don't have any money, and so sometimes they don't have any place to live, or very much to eat. They walk around the city, and at night they sleep in doorways, or on park benches, or in the subways."

"Not in a bed?" asked Tom, his eyes wide.

"Nope. Not in a bed."

"That's neat."

"Well, it may sound neat," I told him, "but it isn't, really. It isn't any fun to be poor. They carry all their stuff around in shopping bags, or in big pocketbooks."

"Like my bag lady. She had a big pocketbook and she hit me on the head with it."

"Yeah. But she didn't mean to."

We looked down the path and could see Tom Terrific's bag lady shuffling along, her coat flapping. The Public Garden was crowded with all sorts of people; no one paid any attention to her. After a moment she disappeared from sight beyond a horde of roller-skaters.

"Okay, old Tom," I said, putting her out of my mind, "this is our turf, like I said. So we have to get to know it. Let's stake out a spot — how about that bench over there? — and draw some pictures, okay?"

"Sure," said Tom Terrific.

I took my art supplies out of my backpack and gave him some pages from a sketch pad and a pencil. I started drawing a tree. A Japanese larch. The trees in the Public Garden have labels on them; that's how I knew it was a Japanese larch.

Tom T. drew squiggles and snowmen. After a few minutes he was bored.

"Look at the Swan Boats," he said, pointing toward the pond.

The pond filled the middle of the Garden, shaped like a big pair of spectacles, with a bridge across the middle where the bridge of the nose would be. On the bridge, people stood taking pictures, aiming their cameras down toward the water, photographing the famous Boston Swan Boats as they glided by. Each boat had rows of seats for passengers and was operated by a boy who pedaled with his feet as he sat inside a huge swan, molded with outstretched wings and a tall curved neck. The Swan Boats have been there for more than a hundred years. I remember riding in them with my grandmother when I was very small, on Sunday afternoons in the summer. After she died (peacefully, in my bed), I used to think back to those times when she and I rode together in the Swans. All Boston children have memories like that. Or so I thought.

"That's fun, isn't it, riding in the Swan Boats?" I said to Tom Terrific. "It's so quiet, and all the ducks swim alongside."

"I never rode in one," he said wistfully.

"You *didn't?* Why not?"

He looked puzzled by the question. "I don't know," he said finally. "I guess I'm not allowed to."

I didn't say anything. What could I say? We just sat there for a minute, watching the Swans glide silently by.

"Can I go for a walk?" he asked.

I was pretty close to getting the shading right on my Japanese larch, and I didn't want to quit yet.

"Well," I said, "you can go for a little walk. Not out of my sight, because I'm taking care of you. Just down the path, okay? Not near the pond. I'll walk with you after I finish this picture."

"Okay. You forgot something, though."

"What did I forget?"

"You're spozed to tell me not to pick the flowers."

"Oh. Don't pick the flowers. It's against the rules."

"And don't talk to strangers. You're spozed to tell me that," said Tom Terrific.

I groaned. "Don't talk to strangers," I said.

"I'm not going to. I'm going to go count stuff. I can count to a hundred."

And off he went. I kept an eye on his red turtleneck jersey as he wandered down the path. Some roller-skaters made an opening for him and he trotted through — seven of them, in case he was counting roller-skaters. I kept working on my Japanese larch and glanced up from time to time, watching his little red shirt.

It sure doesn't take long to start to love a kid.

Chapter 6

*B*ehind me, as I sat working on my drawing of the tree, I suddenly heard the beginning of some music: a few notes sliding up and down into scales, then from the scales into a melody I didn't recognize. It was something you would hum a lot after you'd heard it once or twice: a melody that made you want to dance a long, slow dance cuddled up close to someone you liked a whole lot.

I picked Tom Terrific out of the crowd with my eyes, just to make certain where he was and that he was okay, and then I turned around.

Sitting behind me, on a bench, was a black man, the tallest man I've ever seen if you don't count professional basketball players on TV. His legs were sticking out into the path, crossed at the ankles, wearing jeans, and they were so skinny and long that I thought of a giraffe I'd seen at a zoo once. At one end of the legs was a pair of huge white sneakers, and at the other end was the top of a black man with a small beard and a big saxophone. His long, thin fingers moved around on the keys, and his shoulders swayed a little as he played. His eyes were closed.

I think it is against the rules to play a saxophone in the Public Garden. He looked like someone who didn't care about that.

Out of the corner of my eye, I could see the little red shirt, zigzagging back toward me; Tom Terrific plopped himself down on the grass by my feet. I placed the drawing pad on the bench and sat down in the grass beside him. Bearable lay on his back, staring vacantly at the sky.

"Twenty-nine," said Tom T. breathlessly. "Twenty-nine red rosebushes. I didn't count yellow yet."

"Listen," I whispered, and I nodded toward the saxophone player. Tom leaned against me, resting, watching the man's fingers on the keys and listening to the melody. With his hands, Tom began to do a Seiji Ozawa thing, as if he were directing a whole orchestra. I could tell he wasn't doing it to be funny; he did it unconsciously, as if the music had told him to.

The saxophone player, who had opened his eyes, glanced over, saw Tom T. directing him, winked, and kept on playing. Without a pause, he slid from the unfamiliar melody into something I recognized, though I couldn't think of the words. Tom Terrific could. He began to sing, in a high clear voice.

> Hush little baby, don't say a word
> Papa's gonna buy you a mockingbird . . .

With one hand stroking his glassy-eyed stuffed bear, old Tom sang it all the way through, verse after verse, his little voice right on pitch, even when the musician took the melody and sent the notes soaring around, up and down, wrong side out, all around the song.

A few people glanced over and raised their eyebrows. Some smiled. Then they went back to their conversations, their newspapers, their naps. But off to the side, suddenly I heard another voice join in: a voice quieter than Tom's, but right on key too, and with the right words, until the pair of voices finished together, softly, at the end:

> Hear, oh hear the night bird call;
> Soon, oh, soon the dark will fall.

The saxophone player sent the sound swirling in circles into the bright blue air, then tapered it off and let it die. He took the instrument away from his lips and grinned, first at me and Tom

Terrific; then he turned and grinned in the direction of the second voice. I looked. It was the bag lady, the one who had whomped Tom's head.

Her shoes were tied now, but her coat still flapped around her, and her hair still flew from its hairpins in gray strands and wisps. It was she who had been singing the ancient lullaby with Tom. Now she muttered to herself, hefted her purse more firmly onto her shoulder, and began to turn away.

The saxophone player called to her and to Tom Terrific. "Couple of good singers, you two," he said. "We could get us a gig in a club somewhere, hey?"

But the woman wasn't listening; she had turned and was shuffling down the path. Tom Terrific scratched a mosquito bite on his ankle and said shyly, "I know lots of songs."

"Me too," said the tall black man as he began to take the saxophone apart and put it into its case. "You come around here a lot?"

"I'm his babysitter," I explained. "We'll be coming here most afternoons. How about you?"

"Long as she doan rain. Maybe we could make some more music together, whaddaya think, fella?"

"Sure," said Tom T.

The musician snapped his case closed and stood up. Tall, tall, taller. His legs unfolded like umbrella handles. He came over to where we were sitting on the grass and stood beside us, his shadow extending out across the path. "What's your names?" he asked.

"Cynthia," I lied, "and this is Tom. Tom Terrific."

The man leaned down, held out his giant, skinny hand, and shook ours, one after the other. "You can call me Hawk," he said.

"Hi, Hawk," said Tom. "You play good."

"And you sing good." He glanced at my sketch pad. "You don't draw so bad, either, Cynthia. Man, it's hot. I'm gonna get me a Popsicle. You guys want one? And where'd that lady go to?"

We looked around, but the bag lady was gone.

"I have to have Tom home in half an hour," I explained, "and I'm not supposed to let him eat stuff. But a Popsicle sure would taste good. Hey, Tom, if I get you a Popsicle, could you not drip on your shirt so your mom won't know?"

"I won't drip," said Tom Terrific. "I promise."

So Hawk and Tom and I walked over to the man at the Charles Street edge of the Garden, the man with the Popsicle cart. We all bought green ones. I paid for mine and for Tom's, and he ate it carefully, holding it out in front of him so that the melting ice fell to the path and not down the sleeves of his shirt.

"Gotta split," said Hawk, after he had devoured his Popsicle in two bites and Tom and I were still slurping at ours. "See you guys tomorrow."

"Long as she doan rain," Tom reminded him.

Hawk grinned his wide, slow grin. "Long as she doan rain," he said. He loped off across the Public Garden, carrying his saxophone case.

Tom Terrific and I went for a walk along the path, finishing our Popsicles, before I took him home. It was almost five o'clock. Tom was counting something again. I could hear him murmuring "fourteen, fifteen" between slurps.

The woman in the black coat was sitting on a bench near the Beacon Street side of the Garden as we headed toward the exit there. She was fiddling with her pocketbook and muttering.

"Hi," said Tom Terrific cheerfully to her. "We got Popsicles but I'm not going to tell my mother."

"Root beer," I heard the woman mutter, not looking at us. "They used to have root beer and it tasted like the root beer my father used to make, but not now, oh no, now they don't have root beer ones anymore, they say nobody wants them, they only have green and orange, but they never asked anybody, really, they just decided that about root beer without consulting anyone, they always do that, decide things without consulting anyone . . ."

Standing there, finishing our Popsicles, we watched her for a long moment. I didn't have any idea what she was talking about. She wasn't talking to us, anyway. I think she was talking to her pocketbook.

Finally we walked away, through the Garden exit, to go back to Tom's house. Tom kept counting. "Twenty-one, twenty-two," I heard him saying to himself.

"Now, Tom Terrific," I said as we turned onto West Cedar Street, "you'll have to change back to Joshua when you get home."

"I know." He hugged his stuffed bear and plodded along beside me.

"And we broke a few rules. We ate stuff, and we talked to strangers."

"I won't tell," he said firmly, and I believed him.

Just before we reached his house, he said suddenly, "They shouldn't do that."

"Do what?"

"What she said. They stopped having root beer Popsicles and they didn't even ask her. It was the kind she liked because it made her think about her daddy."

"Yeah," I said. "I guess so."

He tugged at my hand to make me pay attention. "People *like* to think about their daddies," he pointed out.

I sensed then that there wasn't a Mr. Cameron around, only a Ms. "I know they do," I said, and I squeezed his hand.

"Probably they *all* want root beer Popsicles," he said sadly.

"All *who?*"

Tom Terrific sighed. We were on the steps of his house now, and in a minute he would be Joshua Cameron again. "All the bag ladies," he explained patiently. "There were twenty-four bag ladies in the Garden. I counted them."

Chapter 7

*D*inner at my house takes many different forms. Sometimes my mother has to work late at the hospital, so Dad and I eat together; he usually reads the *Wall Street Journal,* and I stare out the window while I chew. Every now and then he remembers I am there and looks up and says something like, "What happened at school today?" Then I come up with some incident from History class, or Gym, which he listens to politely. Or else I remind him that it is summer, or spring vacation, or whatever; he nods, says "Of course," and goes back to his paper.

Sometimes Dad has to work late at the office; then Mom and I eat together. She thinks it is the height of rudeness to read at the dinner table. She talks. She asks my opinion about world news, Boston politics, the weather, or any book by Jane Austen. My mother read all of Jane Austen when she was in college; she hasn't had time to read any books since, only articles about brain tumors.

None of those things interest me. But that doesn't matter, because when I try to give my opinion in response to my mother's questions, she watches me when I talk. Then she says things like:

"I wonder if Dr. McCracken took your braces off too soon. That left incisor doesn't seem quite straight to me, Enid."

Or: "You haven't been snipping at your own bangs, have you, Enid? Call and make an appointment to have a trim tomorrow. You look very jagged across the forehead."

Or: "I really think it's time to bundle up some of your clothes and take them to a Goodwill box. You're not still *fond* of that shirt, are you?"

(It all goes with the name. Enid. Squalid. Sordid. *Putrid*.)

But some nights all three of us are home for dinner. Then Dad doesn't read, and Mom doesn't scrutinize my skin, hair, teeth, and clothes for flaws. Mrs. Kolodny wears a clean white apron; she sets the table with grandmother's silver and lights candles. We have Conversation.

Here is what Conversation sounded like that night at my house:

Me: "This afternoon I babysat for this really cute little boy who lives over on West Cedar Street."

Dad: "Where on earth did Mrs. Kolodny buy this beef, Evelyn? It's like shoe leather."

Mom: "I assume you saw this morning's *Boston Globe*. Can you imagine *nurses* threatening to strike? It's an absolute outrage."

Me: "His name is Joshua Warwick Cameron the Fourth. How about *that* for an outrage?"

Dad: "This beef is an outrage. Did she get this at DeLuca's? Enid, go out to the kitchen and get me a steak knife. You shouldn't need a steak knife to cut roast beef."

(Enid exits, stage left, to kitchen. Enid returns, with steak knife.)

Mom: "What ever happened to *humanity,* anyway? If those nurses go on strike, who's going to suffer? The patients, that's who."

Dad: "I was served better beef than this in the army, in 1951, in Korea."

Me: "I'm going to take care of him every afternoon, from three to five, if the weather's decent. I'll take him out for walks and to the Public Garden and stuff."

Mom: "And can you guess what their so-called

grievance is? That they weren't consulted about the changes in scheduling. How on earth can the administration consult every single employee in a hospital, for heaven's sake? Scheduling is an administrative decision."

Then a weird thing began to happen. Up until that moment, the conversation had been absolutely boring to me. I didn't care about the texture of the beef; mine seemed just fine. And I didn't care about the administrative problems of the hospital where my mother works. But all of a sudden, a little bell began to go off in my head. It was dinging "Root beer. Root beer. Root beer." I looked up from my plate.

Dad (laying down his knife and fork): "Enough. I have to battle with partners and clients all day long. I'm not going to fight with roast beef on top of that. I'm going to go watch the news. Speak to that woman about the purchasing of meat, Evelyn."

Exit Father, stage right.

Then Mom and I were alone at the dinner table. She took one last bite of baked potato, sighed, and pushed her plate a little bit away from her. She looked tired and exasperated. But for once the exasperation wasn't focused on me.

"Mom," I said, "what would happen if just *one* nurse complained about the changes in schedules?"

"One nurse? Nothing. She'd be told to take it or leave it. They can always replace one nurse."

"What's going to happen if all the nurses go on strike?"

She sighed again. "They'll negotiate. The hospital can't function with all the nurses out. Eventually they'll come to some satisfactory arrangement. In the meantime, I have several patients who . . ."

She went on talking, but I stopped listening. My mind was off in the world of root beer Popsicles. Okay; so root beer Popsicles aren't as important as people lying in hospital beds; I know that. But the principle seemed the same. I kept thinking of that old woman, sitting all alone on a park bench with her worldly goods in a big black pocketbook and maybe no place to sleep that night except in a doorway, and I could hear her muttering, "They never asked anybody really, they decide things without consulting anyone, they always do that . . ."

Maybe it wasn't as important in the great scheme of things as nurses, whose schedules had been changed without anyone consulting them.

Maybe it wasn't as life-and-death as people in hospital beds, people who were sick and needed nurses to bring their medicine and take their temperature and maybe just talk to them a little bit if they were scared.

But it was the same basic thing. It was comfort. What if all you had in the whole world, besides a black bag and a chilly doorway, was a memory of a father who once made root beer, and sometimes a Popsicle that brought that memory back? And what if they took that little bit of comfort away without asking you?

One old lady. As Mom said, one person complaining means nothing. Take it or leave it, they would say. But if a *lot* of people went on strike . . .

And Joshua Warwick Cameron IV, Tom Terrific, champion counter, bless him, had told me that there were twenty-four bag ladies in the Public Garden.

After dinner was over and Mom went into the study to watch the news with Dad, I wandered out to the kitchen to visit with Mrs. Kolodny while she cleaned up the dishes. She was puttering around, humming, and she had all the machinery running: the dishwasher, the garbage disposal, even the washing machine and dryer.

Mrs. Kolodny says she likes to run the machinery; it makes her feel like Captain Kirk in *Star Trek*, gives her a sense of power.

"Hi," I said. She didn't hear me. It sounded like the Industrial Revolution in there, with all those engines going at once. I pushed the buttons that stopped the washing machine and dryer, then the switch for the garbage disposal, and finally she turned around, startled by the silence. Only the dishwasher was churning away now.

"Oh," she said. "Hi. You didn't eat your broccoli."

"I know. I hate broccoli." I flopped down in a kitchen chair and kicked off my sneakers.

"Me too," said Mrs. Kolodny. "You want some junk food?"

"Sure. What do we have?"

She reached into the back of a cupboard, pulled out two Ring-Dings, and tossed me one. "Don't tell your mother."

"I won't," I said, talking around a mouthful of sticky chocolate. "Hey, Mrs. Kolodny, I want to talk to you about something."

She sat down heavily in the opposite chair and unwrapped her Ring-Ding. "You ever read *Jane Airy?*" she asked.

I told you already that Mrs. Kolodny is a

reader. Almost every afternoon she goes over to Newbury Street, to the secondhand paperback bookstore.

But I haven't told you what she looks like. Mrs. Kolodny is without a doubt the most *colorful* person I know. Her hair is blue. Honestly. She dyes it that color; she told me so. It's actually white, but once, years ago, she put on some stuff to "brighten up the white" — that's what the label said it was supposed to do — and her hair turned blue. And she liked it. So now she uses the same stuff, once a month, and dyes her hair blue.

Her skin is sort of yellow-gray. Her nose is bright red, and the whites of her eyes are pink. Through her support stockings, you can see that her legs are crisscrossed with knotted purple veins.

She's an honest-to-God human rainbow.

My mother says that with the exception of the blue hair, which is just an idiotic idiosyncrasy, everything else is a visible symptom of a serious illness. I heard her tell Mrs. Kolodny that once. She wanted her to make an appointment with an internist.

"You have visible symptoms," I heard my mother say, "of liver damage, high blood pressure, and inefficacy of the peripheral vascular system. I want you to go to Dr. Goldberg for a complete check-up. You are a seriously ill woman."

"Dr. Crowley," Mrs. Kolodny said huffily, "do I get the housework done to your satisfaction?"

"Yes," said my mother.

"Then you and I got no problem. The housework you can complain about if you want. My body, that's *my* problem, not yours."

"But — " said my mother.

"Butt out," said Mrs. Kolodny.

If I ever told my mother to butt out, she would hustle me off to Wilma Sandroff's office for intensive therapy, and I would have "hostile interpersonal relationships" stamped forever on a chart.

But nobody hustles Mrs. Kolodny.

"No," I said to her, licking frosting off my fingers, "I never read *Jane Airy*. I never heard of it. Lend it to me if it's any good. Listen, I want to ask you a personal question."

She tensed up. She doesn't like personal questions. Her bloodshot eyes narrowed to slits and she looked at me very suspiciously.

"How much does my father pay you?" I asked. "Just in general terms. Do you consider yourself well paid?"

She relaxed. She didn't consider money too personal. "Yeah," she said. "He pays me enough."

"Well," I asked, "what if he didn't? What would you do if you thought he wasn't paying you enough? Or if you didn't like the working conditions?"

She shrugged and began licking frosting off her own fingers. "I'd tell him so," she said. "Listen, in that *Jane Airy* book — "

"Wait a minute," I interrupted. "What if you told him so and he said, 'Tough'? Then you'd be out of a job, right?"

"I suppose," she said with a sigh. The sigh meant: so what?

I was getting excited. "You'd be out of a job because they could get another housekeeper, right? But what if they *couldn't?* What if every housekeeper on Marlborough Street — no; every housekeeper in *Boston* — got together, and they all said they wouldn't work unless everybody's pay was raised?"

Now she looked suspicious again. "Look, Enid, if you're trying to get me to join some *club* — "

(Notice that name, *Enid?* The sound of it? How it has the same ending as *stupid?*)

"No." I sighed. "It was just hypothetical. I've

just been thinking about something. About the power that people have if they band together."

Mrs. Kolodny heaved herself to her feet. "I'm not the banding-together sort. You want to band me together with someone, it better be tall, dark and handsome. Listen, in *Jane Airy,* she goes to work for this guy named Mr. Rochester. Now this Mr. Rochester, he —"

"You mean *Jane Eyre!*" I said. "Sure, I read that in school! That's a pretty good book!"

"Don't tell me how it comes out," she warned. "I'm just getting to the good part now. But listen, if I ever want a different job, that's the kind of job I want, with a guy like Mr. Rochester."

I got up and headed toward the kitchen door. I could tell she was dying to turn all her machinery back on. "I wasn't really talking about jobs, anyway," I said. "I was sort of talking about root beer Popsicles."

But she didn't hear me. All the engines were chugging away again, and she was humming at the top of her voice. A love song. Mrs. Kolodny, the Technicolor lady, is a real romantic at heart. Wait till she reads further and finds out what Mr. Rochester has locked away upstairs.

Chapter 8

*B*earable would be staying home today, Tom Terrific said. He had come down with polio. So we were minus Bearable and heading down the front steps of his house when the door opened and his mother called us back.

"Here, Enid," she said. "Excuse me, I mean Cynthia. Take this with you, and maybe you and Joshua can identify birds in the Public Garden."

She handed me a book and I glanced at the title. *A Field Guide to the Birds.* I stood there looking a little puzzled.

"I heard him as you were going out the front door," she explained, "asking if Hawk would be there today."

I laughed nervously and put the book into my backpack with my sketch pad and pencils. "Oh," I said. "He was probably thinking of a robin or a pigeon or something."

Tom Terrific was down on the brick sidewalk, examining a caterpillar who was trying to make it to his destination without getting squooshed. He looked up, overhearing us, and said, "It was a pigeon. I only said hawk for a joke." He squatted, picked up the fuzzy caterpillar carefully, and deposited it on the roots of a sturdy tree that was growing out of a rectangle of dirt near the curb.

"Joshua!" called his mother in concern. "Nasty, nasty, nasty! Cynthia, do you have a Kleenex? Wipe his hands off, would you?"

I sighed, quietly so Ms. Cameron wouldn't hear me, and wiped Tom's spotless little hands. On the tree root, the caterpillar snuggled into his little yellow furry coat, glad to be rescued from the sidewalk. Probably the instant we were out of sight around the corner, Ms. Cameron would come out with a can of insecticide and blast the poor thing away, muttering "Nasty, nasty, nasty." Then she would go off to pour tea at her meeting of the Save the Earth Society.

"You better watch it," I told Tom as we turned the corner and headed down Chestnut Street. "Don't mention Hawk in front of your mother."

"Or the bag ladies," he replied.

"Or Popsicles."

"Or dogs," he said, pausing to pat a scruffy one that had just lifted its leg against someone's steps. The dog wiggled its behind, trying to wag a stump of a tail, and followed us down the street a short distance until it was distracted by something edible in the gutter.

"There he is!" called Tom, dropping my hand and running ahead of me as we entered the park. "There's the Hawk!"

Hawk was on a bench near the entrance, his saxophone case open in front of him with a few quarters in it, tossed there by passersby. He was wearing the same faded jeans, the same monster sneakers, and a torn shirt that said PROPERTY OF UNIVERSITY OF DELAWARE ATHLETIC DEPARTMENT across the front. There was a hole through ATHLETIC. He had sweat on his dark forehead; it trickled in streams down his face and glistened in his beard. The saxophone glistened in the afternoon sunlight, too, as his fingers slid from key to key. He was playing a song I'd never heard. When Tom plopped down in the grass beside the bench, Hawk winked without taking his mouth away from the sax, and he eased into the melody of "Hush, little baby don't say a word."

I sat in the grass near Tom, took my sketch pad out, and began trying to do a drawing of Hawk. Hands are hard to draw. Hands moving on a saxophone are impossible.

Tom Terrific sang.

Two nuns walking on the path stopped, listened, consulted each other in whispers, and finally tossed a dollar bill into the saxophone case. They walked on, giggling.

When the song ended, Hawk put his saxophone down carefully on the bench and wiped his face with a wrinkled handkerchief. "It's hot, man," he said. "Popsicle time. Popsicles on me today. You earned me a buck, Terrific."

A shadow fell across my open sketch pad, and I turned. The same bag lady, in her black coat, was blotting out the sun as she stood there watching us.

"Hawk," I said as quietly as I could, nodding toward the bag lady, "why don't you play one more before we get Popsicles? You have an audience, I think."

He murmured, "Right." He picked up his instrument and started into what I recognized as "Stardust." Terrific didn't know the words to that. He lay back in the grass, his arms folded behind his head, and listened with his eyes closed. Behind us, the bag lady hummed. I could see her shadow sway in the rhythm of the song.

When he had finished "Stardust," Hawk said

to the woman, "Popsicles all around. My treat."

But she turned, muttering. I could catch the fragments of what she was saying, the same as the day before: "Root beer. They change everything without asking anyone," and with heavy, shuffling steps she moved away, still talking to herself. We watched her go, watched her move down the path to disappear behind some bushes and a statue and the groups of picnicking people, like a huge black bird seeking shade.

Hawk shrugged. "Guess she don't want one," he said cheerfully. "Watch my horn a minute."

He loped with his long, thin legs over to the Popsicle cart and came back with three green ones. We sprawled in the grass and slurped.

"You know what, Hawk?" I asked. "That woman, you know why she didn't want a Popsicle? She told Tom and me yesterday."

"She didn't really tell *us*," Tom corrected. "She was just telling. We were standing there, but she didn't even look at us."

"Okay. Anyway, Hawk, she said that they used to have root beer Popsicles, and she liked those because her father used to make root beer, and it reminded her of her father —"

"Me too," said Hawk. "My daddy used to

make root beer, too. I remember the smell. Summer nights, we kids used to sit on the porch drinking Daddy's root beer."

"Well, anyway," I went on, "she said the guy with the cart stopped carrying root beer because not enough people bought them."

"I would," said Hawk cheerfully, licking his empty stick.

"Me too," said Tom Terrific.

"Well," I confessed, "I wouldn't because I don't *like* root beer. But I don't think it's fair, Hawk. There are a whole lot of bag ladies around — Tom counted twenty-four yesterday — and probably *all* of them wish there were still root beer Popsicles. But nobody pays any attention to what *they* want because they're bag ladies."

Hawk was listening intently. He was grinning.

So I went on. It's nice to have someone listen to what you're saying. "But the reason that no one listens is because they don't make a scene. They just mumble, and nobody pays any attention, and they don't even talk to each *other*. Probably not one single bag lady here ever talks to another one, so they don't even *know* that they all want root beer Popsicles. It seems to me that they ought to *organize*."

Hawk's eyebrows moved up higher on his glistening brown forehead. "Like the Teamsters?"

I shrugged. "I don't know anything about the Teamsters. But like nurses at a hospital. If they want more money or different schedules, they all go on strike. Then the administration has to listen, right?"

"Right," said Hawk. Tom Terrific was examining a worm that he had found in the dirt.

"Right," said Hawk again. "Trouble is, the Popsicle guy don't care about the bag ladies' business. Twenty-four root beer Popsicles now and then, that's not going to make him a millionaire. He's probably already a millionaire anyway. You notice he's branching out into balloons?"

I sighed. Hawk was correct. Even if the bag ladies went on strike, it wouldn't have any effect. None of them bought Popsicles anyway. So much for my great idea.

"I have to go to the bathroom," Tom Terrific announced.

"Wait a minute," said Hawk thoughtfully.

"I can't wait very long," said Tom.

But Hawk hadn't been talking to him. "It's true," he said, "that the guy doesn't care about their business. But what if they organized and picketed? Caused a disruption. Then *other* people wouldn't buy Popsicles, and his business would be affected —"

Tom Terrific stood up. "I have to go the bathroom *right now,*" he announced loudly.

"Good grief," I said. "I don't even know where a bathroom is, Tom. Maybe you could just go behind a bush."

Tom looked stricken. He shook his head firmly. "No," he said.

I looked around, but didn't see any signs of a public restroom. "Think you can make it all the way home, Tom? I don't know where else to take you."

"I'll take him," said a voice. "I'm going myself."

We turned, and there was our bag lady again. It was the first time she had ever spoken directly to us. And she wasn't mumbling crazily, or anything. "I'll take him," she said again, quite clearly, and held her hand out to Tom Terrific.

Well, I might have broken a few rules, let him pat a dog or two, given him Popsicles. But I wasn't about to send him off to a public bathroom with a bag lady. Tough to explain that to his mother if he disappeared and I never saw him again.

"I'll come along," I said. Tom took her hand, I

followed behind, and we headed down the path.

I glanced back at Hawk. He rolled his eyes, grinned, waved, and picked up his saxophone.

She was shuffling along at a pretty quick pace, and Tom trotted beside her. In a minute the three of us had reached one of the Arlington Street exits from the park. I still didn't see anything that looked like a bathroom. All I could see were taxis, people, bicycles, cars, and more people. The intersection of Arlington and Newbury was always a big traffic jam.

"Stay here," said the bag lady to Tom, and she left him on the curb. She walked right out into the traffic, her black coat flapping, her gray hair flying around her head. Cars slammed on their brakes. There were screeches of tires, angry yells from taxi drivers, and a whole orchestra of honking horns. She held up one hand like a policeman. In a second all the traffic had stopped.

"Come on!" she called to us. Hastily, embarrassed, I took Tom's hand and we crossed the street. She brought up the rear, and behind her the traffic started up again; a few drivers called out a final insult.

"Terrible street," she muttered. "They ought to put a light there." She took Tom's hand from me and, at her quick, flapping pace, headed for an entrance. I cringed. For the first time I realized where she was going. I *more* than cringed; I wanted to disappear, to die on the spot.

The bag lady was planning to pee at the Ritz.

The Ritz-Carlton is one of the oldest, the most elegant, the most expensive, and the most snobbish hotels in Boston. Movie stars and kings and sheiks and millionaires stay at the Ritz when they're in town. Once Paul Newman was there, when he was making a movie in Boston, and people stood on the sidewalk outside, hoping to catch a glimpse of him.

My mother told me that once an admiral went there for dinner wearing a dress uniform, the white kind with brass buttons up to the chin, and they wouldn't let him in the dining room because he wasn't wearing a tie.

Someone at school said that Shirley MacLaine tried to go into the Ritz bar one night after she did a performance of a play, and they turned her away because she was wearing pants. (The same person said, "So then she took her pants *off*, right there in the lobby"; but I don't believe that part.)

Once when I was there for dinner (my parents take me there each year, on their anniversary), I saw a man wearing a turtleneck shirt trying to enter the dining room. The maître d' took him aside, and after a minute he came back wearing a tie they had loaned him, wrapped around his turtleneck. My parents hissed at me to quit staring, but I couldn't help it; he looked so stupid, and his wife kept glaring at him while they ate. You could almost tell she was muttering, "I *told* you to wear a tie."

I was wondering what they were going to say when we tried to go inside. It was so mortifying that the only thing I could do was pretend I was Paul Newman's daughter (ridiculous. Would Paul and Joanne name a daughter *Enid?*). I stuck my nose into the air and fantasized that I was going to meet my dad in the lobby.

To my amazement, the doorman, in his dark blue uniform, said "Good afternoon" and held the door open for the three of us, as if every day of his life a bag lady, a little boy walking crosslegged now because he was about to wet his pants, and a fourteen-year-old girl in jeans came sweeping through.

Apparently the bag lady had done this before because she knew the way right to the john. It was just in time for Tom Terrific.

When we came back out of the hotel, the doorman was helping a Japanese man take about thirty-seven leather suitcases out of a taxi, so he couldn't hold the door for us again. But he nodded, said "Good afternoon" a second time, and didn't blink an eye as the bag lady went into her death-defying traffic-stopping number once more.

Then we were back in the safety of the Public Garden.

"Thank you," I said to her. "You really saved Tom's life. Or at least his dignity."

"Who's the Negro?" she muttered abruptly.

I looked around, startled. There were lots of black people in the Garden; there were Chinese, Puerto Ricans, WASPs, and anybody else you could think of. I didn't know who she was talking about. And I hadn't heard anybody say "Negro" for about ten years, except maybe my great-aunt Eleanor, who tends to use obsolete language. Every time she comes to visit she asks, "Enid, do you have a beau?" and for a minute I think she's asking about a hair ribbon.

"What?" I asked the bag lady. "I'm sorry; I don't know who you mean."

"With the *instrument*," she said brusquely.

Oh. Of course. "His name is Hawk," I said.

"You tell him," she muttered, looking at the ground, "I'll do it. I think it's a good idea, it would serve them right, nobody ever fights back, I'll do it if he will, if other people will, you tell him."

"You'll do *what?*" I asked, puzzled. My I.Q. isn't all that monumental. Enid almost rhymes with *stupid,* of course.

She looked up, her little eyes bright and piercing. "Picket," she hissed. "*Disrupt.*"

"Why don't *you* tell him?" I asked; but she had turned already and was plodding away, disappearing around the cement corner of a statue's base. High above her, looking out with glazed eyes over his straight bronze nose, George Washington sat with impeccable posture atop his pawing horse. He stared ahead through the trees, his gaze blank. So did all the other people in the Garden as the bag lady shuffled past them, their eyes like the blind eyes of statues.

When we got back to our corner of the park, Hawk was gone. A man wearing a business suit was reading the *Boston Globe* on the bench where Hawk had been. It was getting late.

I took Tom Terrific's hand and walked him home. He counted things along the way. Twelve dogs, six taxis, and eight bright orange parking tickets on the windshield of illegally parked cars.

Chapter 9

Seth Sandroff called after supper. Probably he couldn't dream up any vandalism that day, and he was tired of tormenting his sisters and looking for someone else to drive crazy.

The Sandroffs live on Commonwealth Avenue, about three blocks from our house. His father owns a TV station. His mother, as I've said, is a child psychologist; but mostly she gets her kicks out of being a Well-Known Personality. She wrote a book once, called *Get in Touch*, subtitled *Living with Adolescents*, which a lot of people bought because, let's face it, a lot of people don't much like living with adolescents, and her book told them how to do it without committing suicide. So she was on the *Today Show*, simpering dumb answers to dumb questions asked by Jane Pauley; and after that she was on a lot of talk shows, and now she is the Dr. Joyce Brothers of the parental world.

She's a first-class phony. One of the things her

book harps on is "learning to love yourself," after which, of course, you will "learn to love your teenager," following which your teenager will, presumably, learn to love you. Wilma Sandroff loves herself so much that as soon as she became a TV personality, she went off to a beauty farm to lose twenty pounds; then she had her hair bleached platinum blond; then she had a facelift. Now, instead of looking like a forty-five-year-old woman, she looks like a Miss America contestant about to do a flaming-baton routine to the accompaniment of "I Feel Pretty."

She loves her teenagers so much that once, in front of three of his friends (who later told me about it), she told Seth that his acne made his face look like a piece of volcanic rock. Seth loves her so much that when she said it, he threw an algebra book at her.

Seth is in my class at the Carstairs School, and his sisters are in the seventh grade. Seth's sisters are twins. Despite the fact that one of Wilma Sandroff's book chapters is titled "Your Kids Are Individuals," she named the twins — ready for this? Got an airsick bag handy? — Arlene and Marlene, and she made them dress identically until last year, when they were eleven. Last year they were picked up for shoplifting in Hit or

Miss. They were shoplifting non-identical clothes. The social worker assigned to the case suggested to the Famous Dr. Sandroff that maybe she should let them dress the way they want (precisely the same suggestion that Dr. Sandroff had made to one million parents in her book). Now the twins dress the way they want, which outside of school is mostly in punk rock style, and they call their mother Plasticface behind her back — or to her face, when her face is looking out of the TV screen. The twins plan to run away as soon as they're old enough to get waitress jobs in some remote state where they can never be found.

Everybody at the Carstairs School knows about the Sandroff twins' plan to run away. There is even a movement afoot, headed by Seth, to hold a bake sale to raise money for identical bus fares to Montana. But Wilma Sandroff doesn't know about it because she is always off appearing on talk shows, telling people how to get in touch with their adolescents. Arlene and Marlene plan to get in touch with *her* someday, by postcard with no return address.

I feel sorry for Seth, but it's almost impossible to like him. His personality is like a rattlesnake's. When I recognized his voice on the phone, I recoiled a little, as if he might strike with poison fangs right through the wires. Somehow even his "Hello" sounded sarcastic.

"So, what are you doing this summer, Enid?" Seth asked.

"Not much. All my friends are off at camp. Trina Bentley's at horse camp, and Emily Wentworth's at tennis camp, and —" I stopped. It occurred to me that Trina and Emily wouldn't want me telling anything about them to gross Seth Sandroff.

"I'm taking art classes at the museum," I added, "and babysitting. What are you doing this summer, Seth?"

"Working at the station. They had to give me a job because my father owns it. But I like it okay." Seth was talking about his father's TV station.

My eavesdropping mother appeared in the hall, where I was talking on the phone. She'd apparently been listening from the living room.

"Is that Seth Sandroff?" she whispered loudly. "Ask him if he'd like to come over for dinner some night."

My mother is actually a Wilma Sandroff *fan.* She has an autographed copy of that asinine book. I made a hideous face at her and formed the words "Go away" silently with my mouth. My mother shrugged and went away.

"— pretty sneaky," Seth was saying. I hadn't heard the first part because of my mother.

"What? What's pretty sneaky?" I asked. "I didn't hear what you said."

Seth laughed, an evil sort of laugh. "I said I *know* what you've been doing, Enid. And who you're hanging out with." His voice sounded like those guys in old movies, the ones who say, "We *know* you have the secret formula, heh-heh."

I tried to figure out what he meant. The people in my art class are mostly kids from suburban schools, kids I hardly know at all. They seem nice enough, most of them. But I don't hang out with them.

"What are you talking about, Seth?" I asked in a bored voice.

He lowered his voice to make it sound really subversive. "I've seen you, Enid. I was on my bike, heading over to Tremont Street on an errand for the station manager, and I saw you in the Public Garden, hanging out with that black guy. He's practically old enough to be your father."

I groaned. But I lowered my voice, too, in case my mother was still spying. I didn't want my par-

ents to know about Hawk; it was just too complicated. "That's just a *friend,* Seth —"

He laughed his sinister, knowing laugh.
"That's what they all start out thinking," he said.

"All *who?*"

"Young girls who come to Boston and meet
these guys in the parks. Seems like a simple pick-
up at first. I saw this TV show about it. A docu-
mentary; we have it on tape down at the station.
These older guys befriend them, maybe loan
them a little money —"

I thought of Hawk, buying me and Tom Terrific each a green Popsicle. He hadn't said it was a
loan.

Seth was going on and on. "Then before they
know it, they're trapped. Hooked on heroin,
probably. Owing hundreds of dollars. So they go
to work for the guy. There they are, prostitutes,
only fourteen years old. Three weeks before,
they were innocent little cheerleaders, back in
Ohio —"

"Knock it off, Seth."

"Eventually their bodies are found, in ware-
houses and culverts. Needle marks on their arms.
Knife scars. One of them was disemboweled; they
couldn't show it on the film, it was too gruesome.

The detective who found her had tears rolling down his cheeks during the interview. 'She could have been my own little girl,' he said —"

"Seth," I said furiously. "You. Are. Such. A. CREEP."

His voice changed from the sinister whisper to an arrogant, know-it-all sort of voice. "You may think I'm a creep," he said. "But your parents won't think I'm a creep when I come over there wearing a clean shirt in order to *warn* them about what the future holds for their precious, brainy, artistically talented little girl."

Now I was really mad. "You wouldn't," I said.

"Wouldn't I?" He laughed. "Unless —"

"Unless what?" He was going to blackmail me in some way. I could hear it coming.

"Meet me at your corner in fifteen minutes," said Seth. "We'll walk over to Florian's and get a couple of those fruit drinks."

The Café Florian sells these great drinks in summer: fresh fruit all zapped in a blender.

"Those are *expensive*, Seth." I groaned. "If you're going to blackmail me, couldn't you start small, maybe with a Coke?"

"Don't sweat it," said Seth. "I'll pay. Fifteen minutes, at your corner." He hung up.

I went to my room and combed my hair and

put on a sweater. Then I went back downstairs to tell my parents that I was going to meet a black-mailer in order to persuade him not to let them know that I was about to be part of the white-slave traffic, seduced by a strange man I'd met in the Public Garden, that I would probably be hooked on heroin quite soon, that they would likely never see me again.

"I'm meeting Seth," I said casually. "We're going over to the Café Florian for a little while."

"That's nice, dear," said my mother, looking up briefly from a medical journal.

"Be home by ten," said my father, adjusting the color on the TV.

Seth was waiting on the corner when I got there, his body kind of draped against a tree. He's skinny, all arms and legs, and he was wearing cut-off jeans and a tee shirt, which made his arms and legs more visible than they are during the school year. Our school has a dress code: jackets and ties for the guys; skirts or dresses for the girls. We all look like a bunch of corporation executives during school. Even our hair has to be neat. After the movie *"10"* came out, Trina Bentley came to school with her hair like Bo Derek's, in a million miniature braids decorated with beads, and she was sent home to undo it, even though it had cost forty-five dollars to have it done that way. Then there was a big flap because the three black girls in the Upper School argued that *they* should be able to wear their hair Bo Derek style since that was an authentic Afro-American style. Finally there was a compromise: braids yes, beads, no. By the time they reached the compromise, no one cared; school was about to end for the year, and the styles were changing anyway.

Seth had let his hair grow for summer, and it looked pretty good, curly and thick. He had gotten tan, and his skin had cleared up some since I'd seen him last.

Unfortunately, he still had his usual patronizing, sarcastic look on his face. Also, he has this knack of raising one eyebrow at a time. He raised the left one when he saw me coming.

"So," he said, "the big Enid Crowley. Lemme check your arms for needle tracks, kid." He was doing a bad Humphrey Bogart imitation.

"Bug off, Seth. I'm not mainlining yet."

He peeled himself off the tree and we crossed Marlborough Street side by side. Even though I knew none of my school friends were around, I checked automatically, glancing at the few people who were passing. I didn't want anyone I knew to see me with Seth Sandroff, Mr. Unpopularity.

We crossed Commonwealth, my favorite street in Boston even though it's the street where the Sandroffs live. Commonwealth Avenue has a wide center strip of grass and trees, with benches and flowerbeds. The sun was setting, and everything was bathed in a pastel light. A woman on a bench was jiggling a carriage, rocking a baby to sleep, and reading a magazine. Two toddlers played in the grass while their mothers talked. A jogger passed us, panting rhythmically. A gray-haired man with a pointed nose walked a gray-haired dog with a pointed nose. A Chinese couple was laughing, the girl hiding her mouth behind her cupped hands. Pink-gold sunlight glinted off the windows of the apartment buildings; a soft breeze blew; and I wished that I were wearing sandals and a full-skirted dress of some light, swirling fabric and that I were with almost anyone else in the world but Seth.

He demonstrated his remarkable ability to maintain the mood of a fragile, fairy-tale summer evening by saying abruptly, "The Nerd Sisters went to Fat Camp."

I translated that to mean that the twins, Arlene and Marlene, had been sent to one of those camps for overweight adolescents that advertise in the back of the *New York Times* magazine: "Lose Weight the Fun Way."

"You're really, really supportive, Seth," I said sarcastically.

"Well, at least they're not hanging out in the Public Garden, looking for trouble." We turned onto Newbury Street and headed for the Café Florian. Here there were many more people; a few of the stores were still open, and shoppers carried packages, hailed taxis, and greeted one another on the street. But the pace was slower, quieter, than the pace of the day. Now it was cocktail time. Dinner time. Theater time. Date time.

And blackmail time, I thought bitterly as I sat down with Seth at a small table on the sidewalk in front of the Florian. Next to us, a tall woman who looked like a model was eating a salad and reading a paperback. At a nearby table, two thin, well-groomed men were drinking wine; one was chuckling as the other told an anecdote in a low, gleeful voice.

The waiter brought our order of the two thick, slushy drinks, and Seth paid him with a crumpled five-dollar bill that he fished out of his pocket.

"Now," he said, turning to me, "tell me all, Enid, or I'll tell your parents."

"You're a creep, Seth. What I do isn't any of your business."

But he didn't answer. He just sat there, grinning arrogantly. It was really surprising how much better he looked in the summertime.

I told him a little about Hawk and about Tom Terrific. He interrupted me with a skeptical frown when I mentioned the little boy's name.

"No," I explained, "of *course* that's not his real name. His real name's Joshua. But what the heck, I told him he could change his name, just in the Garden. There's nothing wrong with that. I even change my own name when I'm there," I added defiantly. "I call myself Cynthia."

I expected him to hoot with laughter. But he just kept staring with an odd, quizzical look.

"Well, look," I said. "I really hate the name Enid. You probably wouldn't understand that. Seth isn't such a bad name. But *Enid*—" I shrugged and leaned over my drink. Down at the bottom you can spoon up whipped cream and mashed peaches and strawberries. "Anyway," I said angrily, "it really isn't any of your business, Seth Sandroff."

"Sethsandroff, Sethsandroff, Sethsandroff," he said in a fake voice, kind of imitating mine. The woman reading at the next table glanced up from her book, puzzled, then looked back down and turned a page.

"You make me sound like a Russian general," Seth said.

"Oh," I said, realizing he was right. "I'm sorry. Well, if that bothers you, maybe you can understand what I mean, about having a place where you can call yourself whatever you want."

"Yeah. I guess."

"The thing is, Seth" — I was really getting into it now, since I'd never had a chance to talk to anyone about it before, except for a few attempts with Mrs. Kolodny, whose mind was off in outer space half the time — "nobody ever thinks about what other people want, you know? Like old Tom Terrific. His mother just *announces* what he's supposed to do. It never even occurs to her to ask *him*, or that maybe he'd like to get dirty sometimes, or eat junk food. And, well, here's another example, Seth: your sisters."

Seth made a face.

"Well, okay, I know you're not crazy about your sisters. But they probably wouldn't be half as repulsive as they are, Seth, if sometime way back your mother had realized that they didn't *want* to be cute little matching clones!"

"You like baseball?" Seth asked. "You want to

go to a Red Sox game some Saturday?" That was his very subtle way of changing the subject.

"No. I hate baseball games."

"Well," said Seth sarcastically, "I appreciate your very gracious refusal of my invitation. It did wonders for my fragile ego."

I groaned. "Sorry," I said.

The waiter came over and asked if we wanted anything else, which meant would we please leave so that someone else could have the table and he'd get another tip. The waiter was more subtle than I was.

We walked back the way we'd come. It was dark now, and most of the people were gone from the grassy strip in the center of Commonwealth Avenue. A derelict had settled down on one of the benches, to drink wine out of a bottle in a paper bag and to sleep. It reminded me of the bag lady in the Garden. I wondered where she slept at night. I wondered what her dreams might be.

I told Seth about her as we turned onto Marlborough Street and toward my house.

"So if I can get Hawk to help, we're going to organize the bag ladies and picket the Popsicle man," I explained. "Make him pay some attention to what they want."

"You could get yourself in big trouble," Seth

said, but I thought I could hear some admiration in his voice.

"No, I won't. It's legal to picket."

"Hey! If you tell me when you're going to do it, I could get a camera crew down there. It'd be a great human interest story! They're always looking for stuff like that down at the station," Seth said.

"I don't think we want publicity, Seth. We only want root beer Popsicles for the bag ladies."

He shrugged. "Suit yourself. Let me know if you change your mind."

We were in front of my steps when something occurred to me. I had explained to Seth about Hawk and about my relationship with him, but I still didn't know if he was planning to tell my parents the way he'd threatened to. He hadn't ever given me his blackmail proposition because we'd started talking about other things.

"So, Seth," I said casually, "are you still planning to get me in trouble with my folks? Or am I supposed to pay you off, or what? I might as well warn you that most of my money goes for art supplies."

He looked insulted. "For crying out loud, Enid, I just said that so you'd go over to the

Florian with me. I didn't want to spend the evening watching TV again."

"That's weird, Seth. Why didn't you just *ask* me to go to the Florian with you? I would've said yes." That was a huge lie, of course, but all of a sudden I felt sorry for Seth. That I would have said no was bad enough. But that he *knew* I would have said no was worse.

My sudden feeling of being sorry made me say something else impulsively: "My mother said to ask you if you'd like to come over for dinner some night."

"No," said Seth abruptly, the way I had responded to his suggestion of a baseball game. "I *hate* dinner," he added sarcastically. Then he turned without saying good-by and jogged off down the street, his long arms and legs pale against the darkness until he turned the corner and was gone.

Chapter 10

"*M*rs. Cameron —" I started to say, but she interrupted and corrected me.

"*Ms.* Cameron," she said pointedly. It sort of confirmed what I had guessed, that she was divorced. I remembered Tom Terrific saying wistfully, "People like to think about their daddies." There was nothing I could do for him on that score. But I thought maybe I could do something in another department.

"Ms. Cameron," I said, "Joshua would really like to ride on the Swan Boats. Do you think —"

"Oh, no, dear," she said. "No, I think not. The Swan Boats are terribly picturesque, of course. But the fact is that it's really only *tourists* who actually ride on them. And they're so crowded. You just never can tell, well, what germs . . ."

It figured. People who live on West Cedar Street tend to have a negative view of tourists.

You never can tell what sort of germs they may be bringing from Illinois.

Fortunately, Tom hadn't been in the room when I asked her. He came thumping down the stairs a minute later, very cheerful, not aware that another of his little-boy hopes had just been zapped like a fuzzy caterpillar hit by a spray of Raid. He had a box of crayons in his hand.

"Oh, lovely, Joshua!" said his mother. "Are you going to draw pictures today?"

"Yes," said Tom Terrific solemnly. "Of trees."

"What a good idea! Cynthia," she said to me, "why don't you tell him the *names* of the different kinds of trees? They're all labeled, you know. It would be a Learning Experience. I'm sorry you didn't make better use of the *Field Guide to the Birds.*"

She dabbed his face with a dampened paper towel — to *polish* it, I guess, since it was already super clean. Then she patted his hair into the shape that the barber at Trims for Tots had meant it to be. Finally she kissed him on the cheek, then dabbed with the towel at the place where the kiss had been.

We all said "Bye-bye."

"You do the words, right? And I'll do the Popsicles," said Tom Terrific when we were out on the sidewalk. "I have lots of different browns." He trotted along beside me, clutching the Crayolas; it was the Giant box, the one with a hundred crayons.

"Okay." I agreed. Fortunately I'd already finished that week's assignment for art class: a still life, in charcoal. I'd done it at home, in my room, of an eggplant, a pewter pitcher, and a pear. Afterward I'd eaten the pear and returned the pitcher to the dining room cupboard. But I'd forgotten about the eggplant, and now it was brown and squishy, still sitting on my desk.

The remaining pages of a six-dollar sketch pad were going to go for Popsicle posters. I planned to Scotch-tape the posters to sticks, after they were done, so our picket line could carry them.

Hawk and the bag lady were going to be in charge of recruiting the picket line. They didn't know that yet.

But when Tom Terrific and I reached our usual corner of the Public Garden, I discovered that our partners in crime were way ahead of us. I hadn't had a chance the day before to tell Hawk about the bag lady's willingness to join the ranks. But this morning the two of them were sitting there together on the bench, Hawk's saxophone still in its case at his feet. They were deep in conversation, her straggly gray head nodding up and down close to his big black pillow of hair as they talked.

"We're working out the details of this caper," Hawk announced when we arrived. "Can you guys do the signs?"

I grinned and nodded. So did Tom Terrific. "I have lots of browns," he said happily, holding out his Crayola box. "Not even peeled yet."

Both Hawk and the bag lady acknowledged his statement with solemn nods. It surprised me. It surprised me that the two of them — a black man maybe thirty, maybe forty, years old and an ancient vagrant with her worldly goods jammed into a giant pocketbook — with their different backgrounds, different lives, both knew what Tom meant when he said "not even peeled yet." I knew, of course. But I'm fourteen. I should have outgrown it by now, but I haven't: the feeling that things are A-okay if your crayons still lie in orderly rows, pointed at the ends, arranged by colors, a little rainbow secret in a box, and none of the tips worn flat yet, none of their paper coverings peeled.

Parents don't ever understand that. They

think that when your crayons are broken and peeled and stubby, you can just dump them into a coffee can and they'll still be the same crayons.

I wondered suddenly, for the first time, if Hawk or the bag lady had ever been parents. But it didn't seem the kind of question I could ask.

"You two Rembrandts get to work," said Hawk, getting to his feet, "and we two organizers will go out and give the marching orders to the troops. Tomorrow afternoon be okay? Four o'clock?"

"Sounds good to me," I told him, spreading my sketch pad open on the grass. I had a feeling that we were about to enter battle and that we should be whispering, "Synchronize your watches, men."

Tom Terrific hadn't been paying much attention to the conversation. He'd been removing his browns carefully from the box and lining them up in a row beside the sketch pad. But I noticed that now and then he lifted his eyes and glanced longingly over at the Swan Boats. One was gliding by quite near us, crowded with people: children holding balloons, a fat man aiming his camera (from which he'd forgotten to remove the lens cap; in two weeks he'd be wondering why his film had come back blank) at the ducks and water birds swimming beside the boat, mothers jiggling babies on their laps, teenage couples holding hands, and an elderly woman sitting primly, wearing an orchid corsage pinned to her blue silk dress.

I saw that for a moment the bag lady, too, looked wistfully at the Swan Boat. Then she and Hawk walked away, her shuffling steps speeded up a bit for his sake; his long, loping steps slowed a little for hers.

Tom Terrific sighed as the Swan Boat glided away under the bridge. Then he picked up a brown crayon, frowned at the blank page, and began to draw a huge Popsicle.

To this day I don't know *exactly* how Hawk and the bag lady managed to convince eighteen female derelicts of all ages, colors, and intelligence to gather at four o'clock the following day. "Powers of persuasion, man," he grinned when I asked him, drawing out the word "persuasion" like a sustained note on a saxophone.

"Come on, Hawk," I said suspiciously. "Tell me for real. Don't put me on."

He chuckled and sank down in the grass beside me, arranging his legs carefully, the way a spider might.

"You got to observe people," he said. "I mean *study* them, man. Scrutinize. You got to figure out what makes them tick."

"How can you figure out what makes bag ladies tick? They all tick differently."

"Riiiggghht. So you approach them all differently. See that one over there? The one with the straw hat and the gloves?"

I looked and nodded.

"I been coming here a long time. I been watching that chick with the straw hat a long time. She's *mad*."

"You mean crazy?"

"Nope. I mean *mad*, man. She's mad at the whole world. She's got a billion angries inside her head, hiding in that straw hat. You ought to see that mama kick rocks when she really feels the need to let loose."

"No kidding?"

"No kidding. So you approach her where her angries are. I told her, 'Lady, tomorrow we going to organize and we going to do in the sucker with the Popsicle cart. He's been taking advantage. Tomorrow we get him good.' Her eyes lit up like Christmas."

So did mine, listening to him. He went on. "There's another one — I don't see her right

86

now — she has long hair down her back? Sometimes she has it tied with a string?"

I nodded. I'd seen the long-haired woman wandering around. "Is she mad, too?"

"Nope. She's suffering from a sadness so big inside her it's like a hog with the bloat. Full-blown deee-pression, man."

"What do you say to someone that sad?"

"I said, 'Madam, it won't change the anguished state of the universe any, but I'd like to invite you to a party at four tomorrow afternoon. A little music, a little cheer, a little action, a little celebration.' "

"And that worked?"

"Well, I'm not sure about that one. You can't win 'em all. She started to cry and walked away. But she may show, still. You can't tell."

"And you did that with all the bag ladies? You figured out what makes each one tick?"

He grinned and shuffled his feet back and forth in the grass. "Sounds good, don't it? Trouble is, it don't always work. That's why social workers throw up their hands, sometimes, and become computer programmers. You wanta know how I really did it?" He looked a little embarrassed.

"Yeah."

He chuckled. "Realism, man. That's the *real*

power of persuasion. I offered a buck to each one who shows."

I started to laugh, but then I felt terrible. Most days Hawk went home with no more than a few dollars in his saxophone case. "Hawk," I said, "you shouldn't have. I'll pay, well, half if I can. I've got a little money saved up."

But he shook his head firmly and turned me down. "My treat. It cost me no more than a night on the town: a few beers, maybe a movie thrown in. And I haven't had so much fun in twenty years, man."

He unfolded his legs, stood up, and stretched. "Look," he said with a wide grin.

And there they were. It was four o'clock. Tom Terrific came running from the path, where he'd been playing with a puppy. "They came!" he cried in delight.

They had come: a bizarre crowd of mumbling, shuffling women wearing ragged coats and baggy sweaters, sandals and rain boots and knee socks and Supp-hose, flowered hats and hair ribbons and wigs. One of them was carrying a scroungy cat in a plastic shopping bag; its head poked out, and it surveyed the scene with crafty yellow eyes, but I could hear it purring.

Hawk came over to where Tom and I stood watching.

"Us three," he said, "had better stay here, I think."

"Don't we get to march?" asked Tom Terrific. He'd been practicing marching as we walked to the Public Garden from his house. HUP two three four; HUP two three four.

Hawk knelt so that he was level with Tom's four-year-old height. "We're the organizers, man," he explained. "But it's the bag ladies' war. We're going to stand right here to supervise. Your first job will be to hand out signs. Did you make enough?"

Enough? Tom Terrific and I had worked all the previous afternoon. I had taken them home in my backpack, and today we had taped them all to sticks. We could have outfitted the U.S. Army with signs that said BRING BACK ROOT BEER POP-SICLES. I pointed to the stack.

But Tom Terrific's lower lip was beginning to poke out ominously. His feet were moving in place: HUP two three four. Tom Terrific wanted to go to battle.

"Hang on," said the Hawk. "I forgot your badge." Quickly he took a marking pen and tore a scrap of paper from one of the last pages in my sketch pad.

HEAD HONCHO, he wrote, and he taped the badge to Tom's chest. Hawk told him what it said, and Tom's lower lip retreated. He smiled proudly and stuck his chest out like a marine's.

"Now," said Hawk, "I'll get them lined up. You hand out the signs. Then you give the marching orders, Head Honcho."

And Tom did. He did it terrifically. When every bag lady was armed with a sign and in a line — a straggly, uneven line, but a line nonetheless — he climbed on a bench and called in a booming voice, "Forward, MARCH!" By then we had already drawn quite a crowd of onlookers.

And they marched. Did they march! Weaving, shuffling, muttering, murmuring, the eighteen bag ladies — with a nineteenth, *our* bag lady, right at the head of the line — headed for the Popsicle cart. The man behind the cart looked up and grinned at first; then he read the signs. His grin disappeared.

On the street, a strange vehicle was passing. It was a replica of an old-fashioned trolley car that was used to take tourists around Boston for a sightseeing tour in the summer. In the front, a young man with a microphone was intoning in a bored voice, "On your left you will see Boston's famous Public Garden, established by the legislature in 1856, designed by Boston architect George Meachum . . ." His voice trailed off suddenly. Heads craned from the vehicle, watching the parade of bag ladies carrying their signs. "We'll stop for a minute, ladies and gentlemen," said the tour guide, his voice more interested now, "and see what's going on here."

Standing on his bench, Tom Terrific's feet were keeping time, HUP two three four, and his little chest was still thrust forward.

Behind him, Hawk had taken out his saxophone and was playing "When the Saints Go Marchin' In."

A huge crowd had gathered now. Their faces were amused, interested, enthusiastic, sympathetic, in sharp contrast to the ruddy face of the Popsicle man, which had looked at first amused, then puzzled, next angry, and finally had settled into a mask of despair.

One of the bystanders, a young man in a yellow sweatsuit, had noticed the remaining signs stacked beside me in the grass. "You mind?" he asked, reaching down. I shook my head; he picked up a sign, BRING BACK DADDY'S ROOT BEER, and joined the shuffling bag ladies who

91

moved now in a wide circle around the Popsicle cart.

"Uh-oh," I said to myself when a mounted policeman trotted up on his horse to see what was going on. "Big trouble." But it wasn't. He frowned, leaned forward in his saddle to see what the signs said, and then smiled.

"My dad used to make root beer," he said to no one in particular as he patted the glistening neck of his horse.

An elderly, distinguished-looking man in a three-piece suit stood near me, with a pipe in his mouth. "It's not cricket to picket," he said in a British accent. Then, when he noticed me watching him, he explained, "That's Ogden Nash." He leaned over, picked up a sign, and joined the picket line.

People began to get their cameras out. Around me, I could hear wives say to their husbands, "Get a picture of the one with the cat in the sack!" "Quick, Harry! Get a shot of that lady in the orange wig before she goes past!"

In the background, I could see the Swan Boats slow from their graceful glide until they were almost motionless on the pond. Everyone in the boats was watching the commotion.

It was all over very quickly. The red-faced

man at the Popsicle cart began first to mutter, then to argue and complain; but finally, when the chant of the surrounding crowd — "Root beer, root beer, root beer" — grew louder and louder, he simply threw his hands into the air.

"You want root beer? So I'll give you root beer!" he shouted.

"When?" called the crowd; then that, too, became a chant. "When? When?"

"Tomorrow!" yelled the man, capitulating angrily.

The laughing policeman moved his horse through the crowd until he was in the midst of the circle of muttering, sign-wielding bag ladies and sympathizers.

"Let's break it up now, folks!" he called. "You've won your war!"

He turned to the Popsicle man. "Tomorrow," he said. "That was a promise."

The Popsicle man nodded grudgingly.

One by one the bag ladies and the others laid their signs in a stack on the grass. Gradually the crowd dispersed. The tourist trolley moved on; the Swan Boats began their silent glide across the pond again.

The bag ladies disappeared like shadows, moving singly away from the crowd and simply fading from sight as they shuffled off. Even our own bag lady was gone.

Hawk drew out the last note like a sigh and put his saxophone down. "They didn't collect their pay," he said in amazement.

Tom Terrific jumped down from his bench and asked happily, knowing the answer, "Was I a good Head Honcho?" and I assured him that he was the best.

I left the signs for Hawk, who said he would take them to his car. Then I HUP-two-three-foured Tom Terrific home.

It was a great feeling to win a war. I was beginning to think that it might be fun to start another.

Chapter 11

*A*fter something works out well, you want to talk about it to someone. During the school year, I spend half of every Saturday on the phone talking to Trina and Emily, my two best friends, about the school dances, plays, and concerts that are held on Friday nights. Or if nothing was held at school, we talk about whatever movie we went to the night before.

You just need to relive things, especially if they made you feel good. But there was no one I could talk to about the Great Root Beer Popsicle Strike.

The bag ladies had all dissolved like ghosts fading into the background of a late night movie.

Hawk? He had loped off, same as always, to his battered car, into which he loaded the signs and the saxophone. I had no idea where Hawk lived, where he went at night, who he went home to.

A statue of Edward Everett Hale stands there at the entrance to the Public Garden by the Popsicle cart, with his bronze overcoat draped around him in chiseled folds. He had watched the whole thing, but his mournful bronze eyes had never changed. Man of Letters he may have been — it says so at the base of his statue — but he sure wasn't much of a conversationalist.

Head Honcho Tom Terrific and I talked a bit on the way home; but let's face it, terrific though Tom was, he was only four. His main concern on the walk home was in getting his browns reorganized in the Crayola box and in bellowing out "HUP" every fourth step.

As for his mother, Ms. Cameron? By the time we reached the house on West Cedar Street, Tom Terrific had to change back to his Joshua self: sweet and cherubic, with his hair smoothed down. He affected great delight at the freshly squeezed orange juice his mother had ready, and I concocted a new set of reasons why we had not, again today, drawn pictures of trees.

"Hey, guess what *we* did this afternoon," I murmured to a poodle tied outside DeLuca's as I walked home. But the poodle yawned, then turned to chew on his own curly hip.

All of this is an explanation of why, later that evening, I called up Seth Sandroff. My parents (if I had tried to tell *them* about it, they would have begun immediately to fill out registration forms to send me to summer camp, boarding school, rafting trips on the Snake River, Outward Bound, a cloistered convent) had gone to the theater. Mrs. Kolodny was reading an old issue of *Good Housekeeping* in the kitchen while the dishwasher ran. She had forgotten to add the detergent, but I didn't tell her. I figured the high temperature would kill the germs.

I left her engrossed in an article, "How to Stay Cheerful During a Difficult Pregnancy," and curled up in the den with a Diet Pepsi and the telephone.

"You turkey," said Seth after I had described the afternoon, "why didn't you let me arrange for a camera crew? I could have had the whole spot shown on *Heartwarmers* tonight at seven-thirty."

Heartwarmers, need I add, is a wretched fifteen-minute TV thing dreamed up by Seth's father, guaranteed to make the audience either weep or barf. A hundred-year-old man with no living relatives celebrates his birthday all alone except for a three-legged dog. Blind triplets are taken to the circus for the first time. All of this is sponsored by a very crunchy cereal with no nutritional value.

"The viewing audience couldn't have stood it,

Seth," I said. "It would have overwarmed their hearts."

"Don't underestimate the power of television. You could have been famous, Crowley."

"I don't care about being famous. It was neat, seeing bag ladies grab some power."

"My dad probably wouldn't have used it, anyway," Seth said. "It would have seemed communistic to him. He gets very uptight when people wrest power."

"Right. Today the Popsicle cart, tomorrow the Congress."

Seth laughed. His laugh is surprisingly infectious when he isn't working hard at making it sound sinister.

"You want to go over to the Florian again?" he asked.

I groaned. "I'm drinking Diet Pepsi," I said. "And I ate salad for dinner. If I drink another one of those million-calorie drinks at the Florian I'll have to go to Fat Camp."

He laughed again, unsinisterly. "Well, do you feel like just going out for a walk or something? It's really the pits, sitting around this apartment."

We agreed to meet down at the corner, and I went to tell Mrs. Kolodny I was going out for a little while. Now she was filling out a magazine questionnaire titled "Is Your Home Decor Really You?" She was licking the pencil tip before marking each little box "Yes," "No," or "Maybe." I cringed. I wondered about lead poisoning. I wondered how many years Mrs. Kolodny had been licking pencil tips.

"Enid," she asked when I came into the kitchen, "would you call me —" She followed the print with her finger and found the place. "Would you call me Somber and Serious, Merry and Mischievous, or Calm and Complacent?"

Talk about tough decisions. "Calm and complacent," I said after giving it a little thought.

She turned a page to peek at the answers. "I knew it!" she said triumphantly. "My decor should be apple green with touches of some vibrant blues!"

It wasn't completely clear to me why that news delighted her so. Maybe it was because she was wearing vibrant blue sneakers.

Back she went to the questionnaire, pencil tip in her mouth. I snitched a few grapes out of a bowl on the kitchen table (very few calories, grapes), told her I'd be home by nine-thirty, and headed out.

Seth was sitting on the front steps of a brownstone house on the corner. I wondered what Seth

Sandroff's decor should be. There hadn't been a category for Depraved and Disgusting.

He had a ball-point pen tattoo of a dragon smoking a cigar on one forearm. His shoes — Seth's, not the dragons — should clearly have been condemned by the Board of Health. Wedged into the back pocket of his cut-off jeans was a paperback of a Robert Ludlum spy novel.

"I never knew you could read," I said. "You practically flunked English last year."

"All I flunked was the test on *The Scarlet Letter*," Seth pointed out. "And that was because I missed the third episode on TV. Would you care to match my English grade against your final mark in Geometry?"

Touché. We let the academic discussion go and headed down Marlborough Street toward the Public Garden.

It was beginning to get dark. Funny; I've lived in Boston all my life, but I had never been in the Public Garden at night before. Muggers, rapists, murderers, thieves, and nocturnal rodents: these were the specters I had been warned about, the things that were said to prowl the Garden after dark.

But now, at dusk, there were only a few romantic couples sitting on benches and a derelict or two curling up around a bottle of wine until a policeman told them to move along.

And I felt pretty safe with Seth. No one would want to mug someone who looked as seedy as he did. At the same time, despite his seediness and skinniness, he had a certain confidence about him, a don't-mess-with-me look. We sprawled on a bench beside the pond. Out in the middle of the water, the Swan Boats were chained together for the night.

"Marlene fell out of a Swan Boat once," Seth said, "when she was about three. Or maybe it was Arlene. I can't remember. We were with my grandmother, and the twins were goofing off, and one of them fell in. Everybody screamed."

"Did someone have to leap in and save her?"

"Nah. Some guy just reached over the side and fished her out. The water's not very deep. Muddy, though."

"I wonder how they get them out there to the middle when they put them away for the night. Does somebody have to swim back to shore?"

Seth shrugged. "I dunno. They must have some system. They wouldn't make somebody *swim*, not in this gunky water."

"Rats," I said suddenly. I'd been staring at the

swans, floating there in the dusk, their eyes staring blankly into the trees, when I remembered how longingly Tom Terrific had looked at them, how wistful he'd been as they slid past filled with laughing children.

"Rats? Where?" Seth jumped like a panther on the prowl and looked around.

"Relax. I didn't mean real rats. I just meant, *rats*."

"Why?" He sat back down and tossed a pebble back and forth between his hands.

"This little kid I babysit for," I told him. "He never in his whole life has ridden on the Swan Boats. His mother won't let him."

"It's only fifty cents for under twelve," Seth said, pointing to the sign.

"It's not the money. She's loaded. You should see their house on West Cedar Street. She just thinks the Swan Boats are — I don't know — *tacky*, I guess."

Seth shrugged. "They are. So what?"

I threw some pebbles out into the water, *plink plink plink,* and they made circles that expanded and expanded and expanded. Seth tossed his pebbles into the center of my circles. His aim was pretty good. He ought to try out for the Carstairs basketball team. They haven't won a game in three years, though they tied Milton last spring and lost in overtime.

And now I was thinking about something else as the Swan Boats moved gently against each other at the center of the pond.

"The bag lady, too," I said. "I saw *her* looking at the boats the same way Tom Terrific did. I bet she'd give anything to have a ride."

"So? *She* doesn't have a mother who thinks they're tacky."

"I don't know." I sighed. "Probably she can't afford the seventy-five cents it costs for adults. But that's not really it. You know what it is, Seth?"

He waited.

"It's because the bag ladies all feel as though they're not real people. They know they're different. Everybody looks at them funny and moves away when they walk by. After everybody's treated you like filth for a few years, probably you start *feeling* like you're really out of it, and —"

Seth was looking at me a little oddly. Me, who had treated him as if he'd crawled out from under a rock for as long as I could remember. We both decided to ignore that thought.

"— so you're not going to go stand in a line

full of tourists wearing pink and green alligator shirts, not if you know everybody's going to nudge each other and move away from you, not even if you've got the seventy-five cents and want to sit in a Swan Boat feeling like Queen Elizabeth for twenty minutes.

"It's not fair," I concluded, and I hunched up with my chin resting on my knees. It was starting to get chilly. "I wish sometime when no one was here, all those bag ladies could come and ride around the pond like Cleopatra's handmaidens so they could feel proud, and important, and peaceful, and —"

Seth had stood up and walked away. I thought for a minute that I had started getting too sentimental and poetic for him, that maybe he was going to do a barfing imitation into the rhododendron bushes. Then I saw what he was doing. He was examining a padlock and chain on the dock. If I had been a comic book character at that moment, a light bulb would have appeared in a balloon above my head.

"Seth!" I called in a loud whisper. "Do you think —"

"Shhh," he said. He stood there chewing on his tongue for a minute. Finally he came back to where I was sitting on the bench.

"Could they be quiet?" he asked. "If we did it at night, and they were absolutely *quiet*, we wouldn't get caught."

There were twenty-four seats on each Swan Boat, plus the place where the operator sat and pedaled. I pictured twenty-four bag ladies, erect as royalty, their eyes bright, their shoulders straight inside their ratty coats and dresses, gliding silently, grandly, majestically, around the dark pond, with a breeze rustling the trees and a moon shining down.

"Yes," I said firmly. "I'm sure they'd be absolutely quiet."

"Could you get them all here together at the same time? At night?"

"Hawk could," I said. "He organized them for the strike."

"I need a little time to plan," Seth whispered. "I have to figure out those locks and chains. That's really the only hard part. I can pedal the boat okay."

"Seth," I said suddenly, suspiciously, "you wouldn't arrange for a TV crew, would you? You're not thinking of this as a *Heartwarmers* spot, are you?"

Seth exploded. "Really, Enid! You know who you sound like? My *mother!* As if you think I'm some kind of unreliable creep or something, like she does! Don't you trust me?"

"I'm sorry, Seth," I said. And I was sorry. "I'm starting to trust you. But it takes a while to change your mind about someone, you know?"

"Yeah," he said grudgingly. "I'm feeling the same way about you."

On the way home I asked Seth somewhat nervously, "What would they call it if we got caught? Theft? A felony? Because we'd only be *borrowing* the Swan Boats. We'd be giving them back. And it would be for a good cause."

"I think," said Seth, after he had chewed his lip for a minute, "they'd call it hijacking."

Chapter 12

I've never taken much time to think about Fate. Mrs. Kolodny believes in Fate, I know. "Well, that's Fate," she says cheerfully when her lottery number fails to win, week after week; and I honestly believe that if it ever *does* win her a million dollars, she will say just as cheerfully, "Well, that's Fate," and off she'll go on a round-the-world cruise, wearing a mink coat and her bright blue sneakers.

Mrs. Kolodny also believes in horoscopes, Ann Landers's advice, fortune cookies, and UFOs.

I am not at all sure about any of those things. But Fate certainly did make itself evident that afternoon when I went to West Cedar Street to pick up Tom Terrific.

"Enid," said Ms. Cameron, "I mean, Cynthia. Sit down for a minute. I want to talk to you about something."

Omigod, I said to myself, using Mrs. Kolodny's catchy turn of phrase. She's found out everything: that I changed his name from Joshua; that I let him eat Popsicles, talk to strangers, and touch dogs. That he made disruptive signs for the bag ladies' strike instead of drawing trees and birds. That I'm a dishonest person and a lousy babysitter to boot.

I sat down apprehensively on the beige velvet couch in the living room and inadvertently glanced up toward the high ceiling. Up there somewhere, I thought nervously, was an ax that was about to fall. I smiled the kind of let's-get-it-over-with smile that Joan of Arc probably smiled as they tied her to the stake.

"I find," said Ms. Cameron, "that I have to go out of town on business overnight on Saturday. Now ordinarily I would leave Joshua with his grandparents in Marblehead, but this particular weekend, his grandparents are entertaining a very large group of guests for dinner, and they don't feel up to coping with a four-year-old."

She went on and on, and I relaxed. It wasn't grill-her-at-the-stake time, after all. She simply wanted me to take care of old Tom Terrific overnight. I could hear her chattering about how she knew I was only fourteen, and it was a big responsibility for someone only fourteen, but she thought — and so on.

Liar, I was thinking. Did she think I was stupid? What was this story about going out of town on business? Ms. Cameron didn't even *have* a business. She didn't work. She spent her afternoons, while I took care of Tom, going to do-good meetings, having tea with friends, taking harpsichord lessons, and playing tennis. Now all of a sudden I was supposed to believe that she was going out of town on business. Enid may almost rhyme with stupid, and I may almost have flunked Geometry, but I'm not *naive*.

Anyway, I thought it was kind of neat that apparently she had a boyfriend. I hoped they were going off to Nantucket or someplace for a romantic interlude. I hoped she'd get married eventually so that old Tom would have a father who would take him camping and stuff and let him get dirty.

But of course I couldn't say any of that. I played along. I told her I was sure my parents wouldn't mind, that I was sure I could manage to keep her house and her son in good shape for two days, and that I'd be delighted to stay overnight on West Cedar Street on Saturday night.

And all the while I was thinking: Fate. Fate had set things up so that we could hijack the Swan Boats, not only for the bag ladies, but for

Tom Terrific, who had never been allowed to ride in one.

And Fate had set the date. It was only four days away.

"When you stay at my house and take care of me," said Tom Terrific happily as we walked down West Cedar Street that afternoon, "we can stay up late and watch TV, and we can cook hot dogs with mustard, and we can tell ghost stories, okay?"

"Sure," I said. "We can do all of that." I couldn't tell him yet what else we could do. I had to set it up first, with Hawk, and the bag ladies, and with Seth. I smoothed Tom's hair as he trotted along beside me, chattering about the prospects for Saturday night. We could eat monumental amounts of ice cream. Play Chutes and Ladders. Have a tickling contest.

"Maybe we could call up my daddy," Tom Terrific said suddenly, looking at me out of the corner of his eye. "in California."

So that's where his father was: three thousand miles away. Poor kid. My father may be behind a newspaper much of the time, but at least he's *there*, in my house.

"Tom, old buddy," I said to him, "whatever

we decide to do Saturday night, it will be terrific."

"Yeah," he said contentedly, and he dropped my hand as he leaned over to pick up a worm from the brick sidewalk. We examined it carefully, squiggling in the palm of his hand, all the way to the Public Garden.

It was a gorgeous, bright blue day, one of those early August days that already has a few of September's molecules floating in it. Days like that make you feel good. Everybody in the Public Garden looked cheerful, as if they had just gotten income tax refunds, job promotions, and new clothes.

I had said to Mrs. Kolodny before I left the house, "It's a fabulous day. You ought to go out for a walk."

She had just untied her shoes, put her feet on the coffee table, and settled down with a cup of coffee in front of the TV. On the screen, a woman with masses of red hair was saying, "Pregnant? I can't be!" and a doctor was nodding solemnly at her in response, shuffling some lab reports in his hand.

"Shhh," said Mrs. Kolodny. "That's Suzanne.

She thought it was menopause symptoms, ha-ha."

I watched with a weird kind of fascination. For seven minutes, Suzanne did variations of her "I can't be pregnant!" line. She dabbed at her well-made-up eyes with a tissue. The doctor sorted his papers again and again and said medical things sternly. "You must take vitamins, Suzanne," he said several times.

A commercial came on, and a gray-haired woman began telling a flustered bride how to make good coffee for her hubby. Mrs. Kolodny lowered the sound.

"Suzanne," she explained, "is pregnant because she got involved with the lawyer who's going to defend her son at the murder trial. The son, Lance, killed a drug dealer, but it's first-degree murder even though it was a drug dealer because it was premeditated, and the reason it was premeditated was because the drug dealer had been responsible for getting Lance's fiancée hooked on heroin. She's in a hospital now. Lance is in jail, of course, waiting for the trial, and Suzanne hired this hotshot criminal lawyer, Greg, even though she had to mortgage her home to do it, and then Greg seduced her after they had dinner together to talk about the case and she drank too much wine."

I nodded in a kind of horrible concern for these idiotic people. "Will the lawyer get Lance off?" I heard myself asking.

Mrs. Kolodny nodded. "Suzanne doesn't know this, of course. But Greg knows that Lance has an identical twin brother, Vance. If they can find Vance and produce him at the trial, how will the witnesses be able to say for sure that it was *Lance* they saw with the gun?"

"Wait a minute. What do you mean, Suzanne doesn't know that Lance has a twin brother? Didn't you say he's her son? She gave birth to twins and didn't know it? Come *on*, gimme a break, Mrs. Kolodny."

She waved her hand impatiently. "All of that was a long time ago. Suzanne was in a coma when the twins were born. She had a brain tumor and she was going to die, so they took the babies away for adoption. Later her brain tumor cleared up, so she got Lance back. But she doesn't even know that the other one, Vance, exists."

"How does the lawyer know?"

"He was the twins' father, see. Suzanne doesn't know that, either, because after this brain tumor she ended up with amnesia. Shhhh." Mrs. Kolodny turned the sound back up.

"Mrs. Kolodny," I said as I headed for the door, "it's a beautiful day. You should go out for a walk."

Real life was certainly a lot less complicated than soap opera life, I thought, as I entered the Garden with Tom Terrific. He scampered off and knelt by a bush, to deposit his worm in a new home. Beyond the flower beds, I could see Hawk, sitting on a bench with our bag lady. They were both slurping brown Popsicles, and I grinned; the Popsicle man had kept his promise. I strolled over to greet them and to tell them that we had a new partner in crime, the Russian general Sethsandroff, and that on Saturday night we were going to capture the navy.

Hawk rolled his eyes apprehensively when I described the plans. He leaned back and made a *Whoooo* sound with his mouth. "I gotta cogitate on that one," he said.

But the bag lady didn't have to cogitate at all. She grinned, her mouth full of root beer ice. She swallowed the last bit of Popsicle and said, with her eyes sparkling, "Let's go for it."

Chapter 13

*T*he telephone conversation between me and Seth sounded like something out of his Robert Ludlum thriller.

"Meet me to check things out." (Seth. Low voice, almost a whisper. Humphrey Bogart, maybe, calling from a phone booth in Vienna.)

"Where? When?" (Me. I wish I had a throaty voice and a slight accent from some Balkan country. But it was only me with my mouth full of chocolate chip cookie. I had just gotten home from Tom Terrific's house.)

"Six. The boat dock."

"Right."

We hung up without saying good-by. It seemed appropriate. Spies never say good-by.

The timing was important because six o'clock was when the Swan Boats closed up. We wanted to see exactly how they did it, how they secured the boats each night, so that on Saturday night we could undo it.

When I met Seth at the dock by the duck pond, I was still wearing the jeans I had been wearing all day. But Seth, having just come from work, looked surprisingly respectable and un-Sethlike in chinos and an L. L. Bean shirt. He sauntered over to the bench where I was sitting, sat down beside me without saying anything, looked around, and then muttered out of the side of his mouth, "You got a pencil and paper?"

I nodded and reached into my backpack.

"Take notes," Seth said in a low voice. He was really into the spy routine. I felt as if we should be wearing trench coats and dark glasses.

No one was paying any attention to us. To any observer — even to the mounted policeman who came up the path now and stopped his horse near the dock — we were just a couple of fourteen-year-olds sitting on a park bench. The policeman was keeping his eye on a shabby-looking man who was leaning on a tree, his eyes a little glazed as if he were stoned.

The horse had his eye on a rhododendron bush. You could tell he wanted a bite of it. But the policeman held the reins firmly in his hand.

The tourists in the park were tired now. Earlier in the day they'd been full of energy, folding and refolding maps, reading the bronze plaques on the bases of statues, taking pictures, pointing out landmarks to each other. Now their shoulders sagged and their children whined.

"I *know* we were going to walk back," I heard a woman say grouchily to her husband, "but my feet hurt. A taxi wouldn't cost that much, would it?"

One after another, the Swan Boats glided to the dock and unloaded their last passengers. Two toddlers had fallen asleep in their mothers' laps during the ride; their mothers deposited them, still sleeping, into strollers that had been parked on the dock.

A young couple came running up to the dock, a small, pigtailed child between them.

"Are you going around one more time?" the woman asked the man at the ticket booth.

"Sorry," he said, shaking his head. He set a CLOSED sign up at the front of the booth. The child burst into angry tears and her father picked her up and patted her back. The couple walked away.

Seth nudged me and nodded toward the place at the side of the dock where three empty boats were now moored. The teenage boys who paddled the boats were climbing around on them, removing the small American flags from their short

117

poles and then bending down to attach the chains that secured the boats to each other front and back.

"Take notes," Seth muttered again.

I groaned a little to myself. Seth was too much. He was really getting into this spy scene. I jotted down in my notebook: "Chained together. Small padlocks."

A fourth boat was empty now, and the boys hooked it up beside the first three. At the ticket booth, the man in charge was filling a green wooden box with things: the flags, a clock, some papers, a portable radio.

A pair of college-age kids, boy and girl, went up to the policeman on his horse. They were arguing with each other.

"Excuse me," the girl said to the policeman. "Is there any way to report a stolen purse?"

"Stolen around here?" the policeman asked them.

"About fifty yards from here," the girl said, pointing toward some benches near a clump of bushes.

"What did you do, put it down and somebody grabbed it?"

The girl nodded in despair. The boy with her

said angrily, "Of all the idiotic things to do, Marcia!"

"Did you see who took it?" the policeman asked. He was looking around the Garden; the horse's ears were suddenly alert. You could tell he was thinking: Wow. Action. The horse, not the policeman.

"No," said the girl. "I was reading a magazine, and when I reached for my purse to get a cigarette, it was gone."

"Of all the idiotic things," the boy began again.

"Well," said the policeman in a resigned voice, and the horse's ears relaxed, "you can go report it at the precinct if you want. But if you didn't see who took it, there's not much they can do. It might turn up in a trash can, but the money'll be gone. Was there much cash in it?"

The girl shook her head. "No. But my address book, and my make-up, and my whole class schedule. Now I won't even know where my classes are, and they start next week."

"Come on, Marcia," the boy said furiously. "He can't do anything." He pulled her by the hand and they walked away, the boy talking loudly.

"Think of it as a learning experience," the policeman called after them cheerfully.

Now the last two boats were empty, and the six were fastened to each other with chains. Together, they formed a hugh flotilla beside the dock.

I wedged my feet protectively around my backpack, which I had placed on the dock, and watched the final closing-up procedures. The ticket man locked his green wooden box and put it on one of the boats.

"Do you think he put the money in that box?" I whispered nervously to Seth. "I don't want to steal any *money*."

"Shhhh. No. He has the money with him, stupid," Seth whispered back.

The six boys who'd been chaining the boats together now jumped over to the dock. With the man, they began to pull a huge, heavy chain from the water.

"What's *that?*" I asked Seth in a low voice.

"Shhh," he said again. "Watch."

They unhooked the big chain and ran it through a fastener on the bow of the middle boat in front. Then the man, with the boy, began to pull slowly on the huge wet chain. The entire group of boats moved. There was no one aboard any of them, and it was eerie, watching them glide away from the dock empty, linked together in a group, out toward the middle of the pond.

"That's cool," said Seth aloud. "I never knew before how they did that."

"I still don't," I said. "How does it work?"

"It's a pulley system," he said, talking in a low voice again. "They've got the cable anchored out there, and they can just haul the boats out and in, all together."

"It may be a cool system," I muttered. "But it sure fouls up our plan. I don't want to —" I glanced around to be certain nobody was listening. Especially the policeman. Even his horse; that horse looked smart. For all I knew, that horse could understand what I was saying. I pictured him opening his lips back over his big yellow teeth and saying in a loud voice to the policeman, "Hey, Ralph, did you hear what the girl on the bench just said?"

But the horse was distracted now by a little boy who was scratching his ears gingerly. Horses do the same thing dogs do when their ears are scratched. They smile.

"I just want to borrow one boat," I whispered to Seth. "I don't want all *six*. And what about all those chains and padlocks? This is beginning to seem like a dumb idea."

Seth was frowning. His forehead was wrinkled and he was watching the boats, sitting out there now in the center of the pond, the swans staring straight ahead with their blank painted eyes.

"Come on, let's go," he said, getting up from the bench. I put my notepad, with its brilliant, complicated spy notes: "Chained together. Small padlocks. Pulley system," into my backpack and followed Seth down the path. When I caught up with him, he announced, "We can still do it. I just have to figure it out. Either I have to get out there somehow, and get one of the boats loose, or we have to haul them all into the dock, then separate one."

"But Seth," I said in frustration, "what about those chains? And that giant cable?"

"Bolt cutter," he said.

"What?"

"It's a tool," he said impatiently, striding along so quickly that I almost had to jog to keep up. "A bolt cutter. We have one at the TV station. I'll borrow it over the weekend."

"Seth," I said slowly, knowing the answer, "what exactly does a bolt cutter do?"

"It'll cut that cable," he said.

I guess it was then that I knew we were going to be in very big trouble.

"A *bolt cutter?*" said Hawk. He shook his head back and forth slowly and whistled. "You're talking burglar tools, man."

But he didn't say no. He leaned forward, his elbows on his knees, his head down, his voice low, and began talking to Seth.

It was the next afternoon, Wednesday, Seth's afternoon off, and I met him at the Garden and introduced him to Hawk.

"Hawk, this is General Sethsandroff," I said with a flourish, glancing at Seth out of the corner of my eye to see if he would mind. But Seth grinned. There was something about the whole enterprise that was like a fantasy, and that made the fake names seem okay. Hawk was caught up in it too.

"Of course," he said, holding out his immense brown hand to shake Seth's very ordinary white one. "The fearless and sinister Russian. Honored to make your acquaintance, my man."

Next thing I knew, they were side by side on the bench, their knees practically touching, going over the plans that Seth had concocted. For a minute I felt a little left out.

But I was, after all, the idea person. The plan had been mine. Hawk and Sethsandroff were only tightening up the logistics; and besides, the less I knew about the bolt cutter, the better I liked it.

I sat in the grass nearby, while they talked in whispers, and played a game with Tom Terrific. Old Tom didn't know anything at all yet about what was going to happen on Saturday night. It wasn't that I didn't trust him not to tell. It was, I guess, that I wanted to surprise him with the biggest adventure of his so-far-not-very-thrill-packed life. He was looking forward with great glee to a tickling contest that night. I treated him to a few tentative tickles as we sat there together in the grass. I like to hear his chiming little giggle. But a tickling contest was peanuts compared to our real plans.

"Let us have your pencil and paper a minute," called Seth.

I took it to them, and Seth and Hawk each wrote something on a slip of paper. They exchanged the slips, folded them, and slipped them into their pockets.

I nudged Seth. "Here she comes," I said.

The bag lady was shuffling down the path toward us.

"Hi!" called Tom Terrific in his sweet, clear, happy voice.

"Good morning," said the bag lady. It was odd. Ever since the Popsicle strike, she'd stopped mumbling. Now she spoke up with great dignity. She still walked as if she had weights in her shoes and couldn't lift her feet; her clothes still billowed around her, too heavy for summer; and her gray hair still flew around her head like spiderwebs wrenched loose from a cellar ceiling. But she talked now. And she smiled.

"I think it's time to consult with my lady," said Hawk to Seth and me. "Her and me'll go buy a couple of Popsicles and have us a chat. We have to start mobilizing the troops again. Looks like we just got three days. And we need to set a time."

We were silent for a minute, the three of us: Seth, Hawk, and me. The bag lady had stopped to visit with Tom Terrific and to admire a bug he had caught.

Then: "Midnight," we said in unison.

"Long as she doan rain?" asked Hawk, laughing.

"Long as she doan rain," Seth and I responded.

Later, Seth went with me when I took Tom Terrific home.

"Right here," I explained when we reached the corner of Chestnut and West Cedar streets, "is where Tom Terrific changes back to Joshua Cameron." I could see that Tom was looking anxiously at Seth to be certain he would understand, to be sure he wouldn't laugh.

But Seth didn't. "Good spot," he said solemnly. "I might as well change here, too, from General Sethsandroff back to Seth Sandroff, ordinary adolescent nudnik."

Tom Terrific giggled. He liked the word "nudnik."

"Presto, Chango!" said Seth in a loud voice, waving his hand in a magician's flamboyant gesture.

"Presto, Chango!" echoed Tom Terrific.

Ms. Cameron looked a little taken aback when she saw the three of us at the door. Her eyes narrowed. You could tell that she was trying to decide how to say, "You are not to entertain *boys* while you are babysitting my son."

But I knew just how to cut her off at the pass.

"Ms. Cameron," I said, "this is my friend Seth Sandroff. We ran into him on the way home. Seth's mother is Wilma Sandroff."

The magic words. "Wilma Sandroff," Ms. Cameron cooed in the voice that adults reserve for church dignitaries. "My goodness, you're Wilma Sandroff's son? I saw her on the Donahue show! I just *happened* to have the TV on — I *rarely* watch television."

It's okay, Ms. Cameron, I wanted to say. You don't have to apologize for watching television. Everybody watches television. Mrs. Kolodny never apologizes.

Seth grunted. We said good-by to Tom Terrific, alias Joshua, and fled.

"Tom Terrific really liked that when you said you were changing back to Seth Sandroff, nudnick," I said to him, walking home.

Seth chuckled. "He's really cute," he said. "I like little kids."

"I don't mean to sound stupid — even though it practically rhymes with Enid, I know — but what's a nudnik, Seth?"

He looked at me in pretend amazement because I was so — well, so stupid. "It's a nothing," he explained. "A blah. A moron."

"SETH! Don't call yourself that! You're not a

nothing!" At the same time I heard myself saying that — and meaning it — I was remembering the way I had treated Seth Sandroff for years. Like a nudnik.

He just shrugged. I though of something else. "Seth, what was the piece of paper that Hawk gave you?"

"Oh, I meant to show you." He took the folded paper from his pocket. "It's his phone number. And I gave him mine. Just in case we have to get in touch about Saturday night."

I looked at the seven meaningless numbers written in pencil on the slip of paper. They weren't entirely meaningless; I recognized the exchange as Cambridge. So that was where Hawk lived.

It was a little weird, thinking about where he lived. To me he was just a Public Garden person. A friend from the green place. It made me uncomfortable to think, as I did for a minute, about what his house might be like, about whether he had a wife, or children. How on earth did they survive — or, in fact, did he survive — on those few coins that people tossed into his saxophone case?

"It's Cambridge he goes home to," I said. "I

wonder where the bag lady goes. *All* the bag ladies."

"Maybe it's better not to think about that," Seth said as we turned onto Marlborough Street. "Anyway, we know where they'll be going Saturday night at midnight, right?"

"Long as she doan rain," we said together. Then we both laughed, and suddenly Seth reached over abruptly and took my hand. A little awkwardly, we held hands the rest of the way to my house.

I don't think it was for romantic reasons or anything. I think it was because we were both scared.

Chapter 14

*I*t rained on Thursday, and it rained on Friday. But Seth told me on the phone that he could absolutely guarantee that it was not going to rain on Saturday.

"Howie Friendly says so," Seth explained.

Ha. Howie Friendly (if you need a description; if that disgusting name isn't enough) is the weatherman on Seth's father's TV station. He wears polyester plaid sport jackets, has dyed hair, and his only claim to fame, as far as I'm concerned, is that he can draw lightning bolts, snowflakes, and smiling suns left-handed while he talks.

Apparently he was drawing smiling suns on Saturday's weather map.

"Trust Howie," said Seth.

Would you trust a man wearing an orange and green sport jacket? I ask you.

I talked a lot to Seth on the phone those two rainy days. Mrs. Kolodny began to make a lot of dumb jokes about "Enid has a boyfriend," and then my parents took it up too, grinning a lot, my father tousling my hair (my God, do you know of anyone who actually had their hair *tousled* since 1902?), and my mother suggesting that maybe now I'd like to go clothes shopping. "Now" meaning "now that a boy finally likes you."

If they had only known the truth. The only clothes I needed as a result of my new relationship with Seth Sandroff were black cat-burglar clothes, not what you'd find in the Prep Shop at Bloomingdale's. We — Seth, Hawk, and I — had agreed that we would all wear black on Saturday night. The better not to see you with, my dear.

As for the bag ladies: well, we couldn't tell them what to wear. None of them probably had anything beyond what was on their backs anyway.

And Tom Terrific? Once when I'd helped him look for a sweater, I had seen a little black velvet suit with short pants hanging in his closet beside all the corduroys and ginghams. Somehow a black velvet suit didn't seem appropriate for this particular adventure. I'd have to come up with an outfit for him that night after his mother had left.

It was all set. Hawk and the bag lady had somehow organized the others, and Hawk told

Seth on the phone that there would be at least twenty of them at midnight on Saturday. Obviously we'd gotten a few converts since the success of the Popsicle strike.

On Friday evening, after he'd come home from work, Seth told me that he had the bolt cutter hidden away in his closet. One of the best smuggling jobs since the Hope diamond was stolen, he said. It occurred to me that the Hope diamond was probably considerably smaller than a bolt cutter, and he was darn lucky he hadn't been collared at the door to the station as he left, with an unwieldy contraption of metal and wood wedged under his jacket.

Ms. Cameron had called to confirm that I was to arrive at six Saturday evening because she was to leave for her, ha-ha, business meeting at six-thirty.

I had worried a bit about getting to the Garden with Tom Terrific at midnight. I'm not a nervous sort of person, but for a fourteen-year-old girl and a four-year-old boy to walk the streets of Boston in the middle of a Saturday night, there has to be some death wish involved. At first Seth said he'd come and walk with us. But, much as I was beginning to like Seth, I wasn't sure he would be all that much protection, not at midnight. He was almost six feet tall; but somehow his body had forgotten to add any flesh to those six feet. He looked a little like a gross picture I had seen once in one of my mother's medical books. Its caption was: Failure to Thrive.

Hawk announced that he would pick all of us up in his car. Now it became "Synchronize your watches, men" time. He would pick Seth up at the corner of Commonwealth and Clarendon, a few doors from his apartment building, at eleven-forty. Ten minutes later, at eleven-fifty, they would collect Tom Terrific and me from the house on West Cedar Street. We were to be waiting just inside the door. As Hawk pointed out to Seth, and Seth repeated to me, if the residents of West Cedar Street noticed a black man idling his beat-up car there in the middle of the night, every telephone around would be dialing 911, the emergency police number.

And the bag ladies would get to the duck pond on their own. I worried for a minute about that. But Seth pointed out that they were used to it. Most of them probably slept in subways and parks anyway. They were a little subculture of survivors.

Frankly, I was beginning to hope that we would all survive this.

* * *

I arrived at Ms. Cameron's at six with my back-pack on my back. She took it from me politely and set it on a tufted Victorian sofa in the front hall. I wondered if she was puzzled by its bulkiness, but she didn't say anything. Probably she assumed that it contained a toothbrush, a frilly Lanz nightgown, and a matching quilted robe. Maybe a pair of fuzzy slippers.

Actually it contained a black turtleneck sweater, my newest jeans, which hadn't faded much yet so they were still dark blue, and a pair of dark brown hiking boots. That was as close as I could come to an all-black ensemble. Also in the pack was a navy blue knitted ski cap. You could feel a little silly wearing a ski cap on a warm August night. But my hair is light; I figured I could reduce my visibility by stuffing it into the cap.

I wonder if full-time burglars ever get over feeling silly as they select their burglaring outfits.

It was not raining. Thank you, Howie Friendly.

Now, as for Ms. Cameron and her bogus business trip. For this alleged business trip, she was dressed in a blue silk dress, low necked with lots of cleavage, high-heeled sandals, and dangling silver earrings. She was wearing make-up, which she never wore in the daytime, and White Shoulders perfume.

(Whenever I'm wandering through the first floor of Jordan Marsh, I squirt myself with one of the sample perfumes. Then I rush home so Mrs. Kolodny can guess what it is. If there is ever a TV quiz program where perfume identification is the competition, Mrs. Kolodny can be a contestant and win thousands of dollars. White Shoulders is a pretty easy one. The one Mrs. Kolodny hasn't mastered yet is Lagerfeld's Chloe. I can always stump her on Chloe.)

It made me feel (a) stupid, that Ms. Cameron thought I would *believe* that she had a business engagement, and (b) sordid, that I was dressed in last summer's too-small sundress when she was decked out in silk. Both adjectives, of course, go nicely with the name Enid.

Her "business partner" arrived in a Mercedes; he was handsome in a Marlboro-ad sort of way (though he was dressed up in a dark suit and tie) and his name was Dave Guthrie. She introduced us. Tom Terrific knew him already; obviously he'd been around before. He said "Hi, sport" to old Tom and tousled his hair. There was an awful lot of hair tousling going on lately, if you ask me. When Dave Guthrie was looking in another direction, Ms. Cameron smoothed old Tom's hair back into its neatly barbered little arrangement.

Ms. Cameron gave the number where she would be, I tucked it into the pocket of my backpack, and off they went after she had planted a lot of teeny-weeny tasteful kisses around her son's head and shoulders. She had already given me lots of not kisses but instructions: nourishing supper, dutiful bath, no TV, two bedtime stories (nonviolent), diligent brushing of teeth, lighting of nightlight, and tucking in at eight P.M. sharp.

I planned to ignore all of her instructions.

With great chortles of glee we dumped the little meat loaf and the little baked potatoes and the little salads down the little garbage disposal, which ate them up with little crunching sounds. Then we had a grossly loaded pizza delivered. It cost me nine dollars, but what the heck; this was a special night, and I'd already banked almost ninety dollars of babysitting money this summer.

By the time we had both pigged out on pizza, it was after seven. Four and a half hours to go.

"Tickling time!" said Tom Terrific, and he lunged at my armpits.

We rolled around on the living room floor for a while, tickling and giggling, until we were afraid we'd barf up nine dollars' worth of pizza.

I tried to think of dopey things that I liked to do when I was younger.

"Hey, Terrific," I said. "You want to make some phone calls?"

He shook his head solemnly. "I'm not allowed to touch the telephone," he said.

"You watch then," I told him. "And listen." I picked up the telephone book, turned to a page at random, and dialed a stranger's number.

"Is your refrigerator running?" I asked in a serious voice when someone answered the phone. "You'd better run after it before it gets away!" I said next, then hung up quickly.

Tom Terrific looked at me in absolute amazement and delight. "Did they say yes?" he asked. "Did they say their refrigerator was running?"

I nodded.

He began to laugh. "And then you said, 'You'd better run after it!' Do it again!"

I did it again, twice more, to unsuspecting people, and Tom threw himself on the couch, roaring with laughter. "You tricked them!" he cried. "Let me do it!"

I picked out another number and reached toward the telephone. "No, let me!" said Tom. "I can read numbers. Tell me the numbers and let me do them!"

So he dialed carefully, and in a scared, awed voice he said, "Is your refrigerator running?"

Then, with more confidence, in a deeper voice he said, "Better run after it before it gets away!" He put the receiver down and stood there, holding his hands over his mouth, astonished and pleased that he had done a forbidden thing, that he had played a trick.

He did it again and again until the novelty wore off. By then it was eight o'clock. Less than four hours to go.

"Eight o'clock," I said without thinking, looking at my watch.

Tom Terrific's face fell. "Bedtime," he said sadly. "I was spozed to have my bath at seven-thirty."

At some point I was going to have to tell my little buddy that he wasn't going to bed tonight. I looked at him. There were pizza remains on his chin and nose. Well, a bath would kill a little more time.

"Come on," I said. "Upstairs for your bath. Want to make it a bubble bath?"

"What's that?" asked Tom Terrific.

What's *that?* What's a bubble bath? Can you imagine a four-year-old kid who never in his life has had a bubble bath? Talk about underprivileged!

I tried to explain about the fun of being surrounded by bubbles.

"I don't think I'm allowed to do that," he said apprehensively.

"Tonight you are," I told him, and I went to the kitchen and got a bottle of dishwashing liquid. Great for bubbles.

Watching Tom Terrific's face as the bubbles appeared in the bathtub was just as good as watching the kid in the movie when E.T. appeared in his back yard. Tom's eyes grew big and then bigger, and his grin spread across his face until dimples appeared on either side. I dropped his clothes into the hamper and lifted him, wiggling in delight, into his bubble bath. He squealed with happiness.

For forty-five minutes we played: Tom in the bath, me sitting on the floor beside the tub. I made him a beard of bubbles and lifted him up to see himself in the mirror. Then I soaped his hair — promising a cross-your-heart oath that I wouldn't get soap in his eyes — and shaped it into a pair of devil horns, which I then had to show him in the mirror as well. We threw bubbles all over the bathroom. We drove matchbox cars along the rim of the tub and plunged them into the water again and again, with sound effects.

Finally, when his fingertips had turned into absolute prunes, I lifted him out of the tub, rubbed him with a thick towel until he was bright pink, and dried his hair. He scampered naked across the hall to his bedroom to get his pajamas, and I cleaned the bathroom until it looked fairly normal.

"What time is it?" Tom Terrific called.

I looked at my watch. "Almost nine," I called back. "Why?"

He trudged from his bedroom back to where I was. He was wearing seersucker pajamas, wrong side out, and funny little blue slippers on the wrong feet.

"No stories tonight," he announced with a shake of his head. "I have to go right smack to sleep imm-meed-i-ut-ly!"

"Wrong," I announced as I scooped him up into my arms. "Now we're going to watch *Love Boat* on TV." I carried him down the stairs.

Less than three hours left.

I turned on the TV set and we curled up together on the pale green couch in the study. Tom watched the first few commercials intently, giggling when a dog said, "Yuck, I don't want that nutritional dog food." Then his head became heavier against my arm, and when I looked down, his eyes were closed.

"You asleep?" I whispered.

"Nope," he whispered back, his eyelids fluttering a little. Then he sighed and his head flopped into my lap. He was zonked. I stroked his damp hair while I watched the characters on the show, a rerun I'd seen before, fall in and out of love.

Love Boat ended. Ricardo Montalban advertised a long, sleek car. A rerun of *Fantasy Island* began. Tom slept on. I reached over for a crocheted afghan that was folded on the arm of the couch and covered him. He snuggled closer to me. He smelled clean and fresh and young.

Fantasy Island ended and I watched the news: a plane crash in Hong Kong, a fire in Dorchester, a drug bust in Gloucester. I watched Howie Friendly draw a tornado funnel in Nebraska and some small thunderclouds in Maine, all with his left hand. I watched the Red Sox lose on a third-baseman's error in the ninth. I looked at my watch. Eleven-thirty. I yawned. Tom Terrific slept.

Carefully I removed his head from my lap and lowered it to the soft couch. I found my backpack in the hall and changed my clothes in the small bathroom on the first floor. Hanging on a hook on the back of the bathroom door was a woman's dark blue cable-knit cardigan. I took it back to the study and gently directed Tom's little arms into the sleeves; he never stirred. I buttoned the sweater down the front; it fit him like a strange little coat. I switched his slippers to the correct feet and zipped them up again.

A sports special was on the TV now, and two tennis players were smashing serves at each other at about a hundred miles an hour. I turned the set off and looked at my watch. Eleven-forty-five.

I turned off most of the lights, put the house keys into my backpack, and pulled the leather straps over my shoulders. Then I picked up Tom Terrific, who draped one arm around my neck in his sleep, and went to the front door. I opened it a few inches just as Hawk's car came slowly down West Cedar Street. When the car stopped in front of the house, I opened the door completely, went outside, closed it behind me, and checked to be sure it had locked. I carried the sleeping four-year-old down the front steps, and Hawk reached one hand behind him to open the car's back door for us.

The street was dark and silent except for a few tree leaves, which whispered in the slight breeze.

I lifted Tom Terrific into the car, placed him on the back seat, and climbed in beside him. He sat bolt upright suddenly, and his eyes opened in fright.

"What are we doing?" he asked groggily.

Hawk checked to be certain the door was closed tightly. He pushed the lock button down. Seth turned in his seat and whispered "Hi."

"What are we *doing?*" asked Tom again, looking around in bewilderment as the car began to move down the street.

"An adventure," I told him. "We're going to meet the bag ladies at the Garden. And we're going to ride in the Swan Boats!" I realized I was sounding like somebody's grandmother, full of fake excitement, trying to prod a reluctant child into some dubious enthusiasm: "Won't that be *fun?*"

Tom climbed into my lap and clung to my neck. "I'm scared," he whimpered.

Chapter 15

*H*awk pulled his car into a parking place on the Arlington Street side of the Public Garden, almost across the street from the Ritz. Apprehensively I tried to remember how many hours it had been since Tom Terrific had gone to the john. But the Ritz didn't seem to evoke any memories or needs in him. He was still curled in my lap with his head on my shoulder, but he was becoming more alert, more awake now. He lifted his head when the car was parked, looked around, and smiled a little when he saw George Washington's statue looming palely through the darkness.

The night was clear, beginning to be chilly now that it was August, and there was a thin smile of a moon. An occasional car passed in the street. There were lights in the windows of hotels and in the tall office buildings where maintenance men and cleaning crews did their work on weekends and in the wee hours. On the other side of the Garden, the brick houses of Beacon Hill were dark.

And the Garden itself was shadowed and dim, the statues and flowers luminous and ghostly, the huge trees silhouettes against the midnight sky.

Seth, on the sidewalk, opened the back door of the car, reached in, and lifted Tom Terrific from my lap.

"Here we go, Head Honcho," he said gently. "Adventure time." Tom wrapped his arms around Seth's neck. I got out and closed the door. Behind me, Hawk was removing things from the car's trunk: the bolt cutter (I winced; but it didn't look as sinister as I had expected; it was like a large pair of pruning shears) and, to my surprise, his saxophone case. He saw my startled look and shrugged, grinning. "I never go anyplace without it," he explained.

We entered the Garden. George Washington's horse pawed the air, frozen in his eternal pose, and the general stared blankly ahead as we passed him. His bronze face was focused on his own battles, ignoring ours.

It was a short walk to the bridge that spanned the pond and across it to the other bank, where the dock was. The water looked black and calm, and the ducks that usually quacked and paddled noisily were now sleeping in secret places along the edges of the pond and in the tall grasses that tufted its small island. None of us spoke. Even Tom Terrific, though he was wide awake now, riding in Seth's arms, was silent; his eyes were wide, but his usual giggles and questions were stilled by the night and the sense of mystery.

"Where are the bag ladies?" I whispered to Seth and Hawk as we went down the steps to the dock.

"They'll be here," Hawk whispered back. "They said they would."

Seth deposited Tom Terrific on the bench at the side of the dock. "Stay," he said, as if he were talking fondly to a puppy. Tom curled his little slippered feet up under him on the bench and stayed. I sat down beside him and held his hand.

The Hawk set his saxophone case on the dock beside us. "Watch my horn," he said, as he had said it to me before, in the park. I nodded.

Through the dim light I could see the figures of Seth and Hawk, both bending toward the water at the edge of the dock, and I could hear them murmur and whisper to each other. "There. Grab it now," I heard Hawk say in a low voice to Seth.

Then I heard the clank of the chain.

Out in the middle of the pond, together in a row, I could see the six Swan Boats floating. "Look," I whispered to Tom Terrific, and I pointed. "That's where the Swan Boats sleep at night."

He stared at them, wide-eyed, and put his thumb into his mouth. After a moment he withdrew his thumb and whispered in an awed voice. "They're waking up now."

He was right. The Swan Boats were beginning to move. They were silent, the six long necks of the swans arching in a row, their dark eyes as blind as the eyes of George Washington, their stiff wings spread. Slowly they glided, linked together, toward the dock. The only sound was the muffled clank of the heavy chain as Seth and Hawk pulled it together.

I shivered. So did Tom. I glanced around, but there was no one there: just Seth and Hawk, crouched at the edge of the dock, straining as they pulled, and me and Tom Terrific, huddled together on the bench. The bag ladies hadn't come. I held my wrist up in the pale light and read the time from my watch; it was five past twelve. We had done it for them, and they hadn't come. It was just the four of us now, in this all alone. The chain scraped rhythmically against the dock as they continued to pull. The Swan Boats continued to glide, larger now as they came closer, majestic and mute.

"Here they come," breathed Tom. I squeezed his hand.

And finally they were there, the six boats in a line at the edge of the dock, the way I had seen them lined up in the evening after the last tourist had gone and they were ready to be secured for the night. Now Seth and Hawk stood up and moved silently, each of them to a different task, quick and efficient. I realized they had plotted this out between them, that like bank robbers or a team of surgeons, each knew his job. Without a word, they moved across the boats, unfastening things here and there. I heard chains slip from wood. I watched as they separated one Swan Boat from the others and brought it to the boarding area. The other five, still linked together, bobbed still and silent at the side of the dock. But one was now ours. One was alone and free, waiting for us in the summer night.

Hawk came to our bench and put the bolt cutter down. He picked up his saxophone case. "Come on," he whispered.

"Ready?" I asked Tom Terrific, and he nodded. He took my hand and padded in his soft slippers across the dock, beside me, to the swan.

Seth lifted Tom Terrific aboard, into one of the wide seats, and steadied the boat as I climbed on beside him.

Then I heard a noise. It was a barely perceptible sound, eerie and everywhere, as if the trees and flowers and statues were breathing and beginning to move. Tom heard it, too. He grabbed my hand. We turned and looked at the dock, where Hawk and Seth still stood, holding the boat, and beyond the dock to the shadowy Garden.

Coming now from behind the bushes, statues, and trees, silent and stealthy as ghosts, were the bag ladies.

None of them mumbled or shuffled or spoke. The only sound was that barely audible shift in the atmosphere, the whisper of air that told of figures moving through the night. They came separately, unlike the chained swans. One by one, as Tom, Seth, Hawk, and I all watched, they moved to the dock and gathered there. They were dark and motionless now, like a congregation standing in a dim cathedral.

While Seth held the boat, Hawk helped each bag lady aboard. Watching his tall, thin fingers in the darkness, watching him bend at the waist as he held out his hand again and again to the figures in the procession, it struck me that he was as gracious, as gallant, as respectful, as the doorman at the Ritz, and that they were as dignified as anyone to whom a hand of help had ever been extended.

When they were all seated in the boat, I saw that something had been left behind in the shadows on the dock. Their bags! Each lady had put down her bag full of tattered secrets, and all the fragments of her everyday life had been left ashore when she took Hawk's hand and found her place on the swan. Each of us had done so. We had left our lives behind.

Quietly, Seth swung himself aboard and into the swan seat at the rear, from which he would pedal and steer. Hawk lifted his saxophone case over and set it down carefully. Then he unclipped a rope and pushed the boat along the side of the dock to give it a little momentum. Finally he stepped across the widening strip of water and sat down in the last seat himself. Now the swan was free. Together we all glided out into the dark pond.

I could feel Tom's little body, warm and soft, nestled beside me. Ahead of me I could see the night sky with its splinter of moon and the city looming with its gray and geometric shapes; around me, the trees of the Garden and the smooth dark water of the pond. I looked back and saw Seth's head turn as he glanced to either side, getting his bearings in the dim light; his shoulders were straight and proud and taut with power.

Now I could hear small sounds as well. The breeze. Tom Terrific's contented sigh. The shiftings of the bag ladies as they adjusted to the motion of the boat, and the tiny click of the latch on Hawk's saxophone case. I heard rustlings, suddenly, in the grasses along the sides of the pond: the ducks were waking. With muted quacks and flutters, they slid from their nests into the water and began to swim; I nudged Tom and pointed. Toward the boat, and then beside it, in patterns as graceful and silent as that of the swan itself, the ducks — there seemed hundreds — now moved solemnly with us through the night. I turned to look at the ladies, seated in the rows around me, and although their individual features were lost in darkness, I could see their postures: erect, stately, like the most noble of rulers being carried through an honored populace.

Then, through the dark quiet, I heard the first notes as Hawk began to play. Melancholy fragments of melodies slid around and over us and through the night sky as the swan moved in a long semicircle at one end of the pond and then along the other shore to the bridge. I recognized bits and pieces of songs I had heard him play before; now he was letting them flow, one into the next, a concerto of memories. I could see from their outlines that some of the ladies were swaying slightly with the rhythm of the music. The swan moved now under the bridge, into hollow echoes and deep shadows, and out into the expanse of pond on the other side. Hawk eased the melody into the opening lines of "Stardust." One of the ladies began to hum.

The swan moved so slowly that it felt almost motionless, almost as if the only thing carrying us along was the song, its phrases sliding into each other smoothly until the end. Then, as we came around the curving corner at the far end of the pond, Hawk began the same song again, the same haunting sequence of notes, and the bag ladies began to sing softly.

"Sometimes I wonder," they sang, "why I spend the lonely nights . . ."

They were tentative voices at first. They were the voices of people who had not sung in a long time, who are uncertain, alone, and fearful. But as the swan moved along, so did the song, and their voices almost magically grew stronger; they began to blend together. They became less hesitant. They became a choir.

"Beside a garden wall," they sang in unison, in tune, in a kind of wonderful rapture, "when stars were bright . . ."

I didn't sing. I didn't know the words. It was a song from a different time, a time that had never belonged to me. It was their time. Their song. Their night. It was my time only to listen.

It was while they sang, and I listened, hugging Tom close to me, that I saw the first police car drive up with its lights out and park beside the Garden. A minute later, the second and third. I heard the measured clop of a horse's hooves. Seth saw and heard them, too; he glanced at me. There was nothing we could do, and although we didn't speak to each other, I knew that Seth and I were thinking the same thing: as long as we can make this last, we will. We'll give them as much as we can of this night.

By the time we had glided under the dark hollows of the bridge again and were coming close to the dock, the song had faded away and the last saxophone notes were floating out into the Garden. I think the police had waited, as Seth and I

had, for the moment to come to its own comple-
tion. There was an endless minute of absolute silence, which I hope was filled with memories of
better times and less lonely nights.

Then the spotlights came on. The pond was
entirely ringed now with police. The lights
blinded us in every direction we looked, and
through a loudspeaker a harsh, commanding
voice, said, fracturing the night, "You are all
under arrest."

Chapter 16

*T*here were so many police on the dock when we moored the boat that it looked like a convention of tourists waiting for the next ride. Some of them actually had drawn their guns; I suppose they thought it wouldn't be easy to arrest a group of twenty-five felons.

"I don't believe this," I heard one of them say. "It's a bunch of old ladies and kids." I saw him return his pistol to its holster.

"Cuff the black guy," the voice said through the loudspeaker, and with a feeling of powerless horror I saw two policeman grab Hawk as he stepped off the boat and handcuff his wrists together behind his back.

I was holding Tom Terrific tightly, waiting my turn to get off and watching in despair. There was chaos on the dock. But the chaos was coming from the policemen, who were jostling each other, shouting instructions. In the midst of them, with enormous self-confidence and dignity, the bag ladies were stepping over to the dock one by one.

Seth climbed out of the seat from which he had operated the swan and made his way to where I stood speechless, with Tom's arms wrapped in panic around my neck and his face buried in my shoulder. He put his arm around us both.

"I love you guys," Seth said. Then a policeman who had come aboard grabbed him, twisted his arm behind his back, and shoved him forward, leaving us behind.

Finally it was my turn; they called to me to come forward, and they helped me to the dock without any grabbing or twisting or handcuffs. They didn't take Tom from me. I stood there holding him, a policeman at my side, and watched them herding the bag ladies to the waiting cars.

After a few minutes of utter confusion, there were only a few of us left on the dock. Seth, with a policeman holding him. Hawk, handcuffed, with two policemen, one on either side. Me and Tom, with our policeman, who looked a little disgruntled that he'd been stuck with guarding the girl and the baby. And to my surprise, our own bag lady, who had been brought back from the group, her gray hair flying about her head, insisting that she was in charge of everything. A baffled policeman stood beside her, shaking his head.

There were bright lights everywhere, and I

was squinting uncomfortably, barely able to see. One of them seemed to be coming from a guy holding a camera.

"Names," ordered someone in a uniform, and I remembered vaguely something about the rules of war. You have to give your name, rank, and serial number, but nothing else. I wondered if this qualified as war.

The bag lady had told him something — her name, I suppose — and he wrote it down and turned to Hawk.

Even with his arms wrenched behind his back, Hawk stood tall and proud. "Wilson B. Hartley," he said with dignity.

"He's the Hawk!" called Tom Terrific, lifting his head.

Wilson B. Hartley smiled at Tom. "Sometimes I'm called Hawk," he told the policeman. "Because of the sax."

The policeman glanced up from the pad of paper he was writing on and smiled half a smile before he thought better of it. "I'm a Coleman Hawkins fan myself," he said gruffly.

"Now you," he said, turning to Seth. "Name."

"Seth Andrew Sandroff."

"Oh, no," groaned the man with the camera. "It's the Sandroff kid. The boss's son! We'll never be able to use this!"

"And you," the policeman said to me, ignoring the TV cameraman. "Name."

"Cynthia," I mumbled miserably, thinking: Enid. Stupid. Sordid. Putrid. Squalid. Rancid. "Cynthia," I said more clearly. "Cynthia Crowley."

"And the kid?"

Tom Terrific held his head high and looked him in the eye, not even squinting in the bright lights. "I'm Tom Terrific," he said in a loud, clear voice.

The policeman's ball-point pen stopped in mid-air.

"Just a minute," said Seth. "Let me speak to him." He moved toward Tom, the policeman still holding his arm firmly.

"Tom," said Seth gently, "it's Presto Chango time, remember?"

Tom nodded solemnly. "Presto Chango," he said. Then he looked at the policeman again. "My name is Joshua Cameron," he announced, and the policeman wrote that down.

"Whose kid is he?"

I sighed. "In my backpack I have the phone number where you can reach his mother."

They wouldn't let me get it myself. Maybe

they thought I had a weapon in there. Someone went through the pack, found the slip of paper, and went off to one of the police cars.

"What did you do, *steal* this kid?" asked the policeman.

It struck me as ridiculous that we were all standing there beside a very large boat that we had *obviously* stolen, and instead of asking about that, they were more concerned with a sleepy, gutsy kid who'd just had the night of his life.

"I guess I borrowed him" was the only answer I could think of. Unfortunately there were reporters gathered by then, and they heard me. "I guess I borrowed him" was the subheadline in the *Herald-American* the next morning. It came under the disgusting headline: TEENS HEIST HILL HEIR.

The "teens," of course, were me and Seth. The "Hill Heir" was Tom Terrific, who, according to the *Herald* story, was heir to the Cameron fortune, whatever that might be.

I only saw the newspaper the next day because Mrs. Kolodny smuggled it up to me in my bedroom, to which I'd been banished. My parents weren't speaking to me at that point. They'd had to come to police headquarters in the middle of the night.

So, of course, did Seth's. But his father came alone. His mother was conducting a seminar on Love and Discipline in San Diego while her only son was heisting the Hill Heir in Boston.

I don't know who came to get Hawk (Wilson B. Hartley, though it was hard for me to think of him by that name). And I don't know who came to get the bag lady.

But I know who both of them are, now, because of the newspaper.

"Omigod, Enid," said Mrs. Kolodny when she brought the paper upstairs. "How did you ever meet those people?"

"They're not bad people," I told her. "They're just poor, Mrs. Kolodny. You've got to get over that bigoted notion that poor people are *bad*." I frowned and took the paper from her; it was creased and folded so that you couldn't miss the awful picture on the front page: the Swan Boat floating, empty, by the dock; policemen milling around; Hawk's gaunt face staring out over the tops of everyone's heads; my back, my hair a mess; and Tom Terrific's little head leaning on my shoulder. You couldn't see Seth or the bag lady.

"I don't know what you mean about *poor*," muttered Mrs. Kolodny. "Here. Read. What'd

160

that lady want to get mixed up in such craziness for?"

I read. I read the bag lady's name: Julia Simpson Forbes. I read her address. She lived in the penthouse at the Ritz. She'd lived there ever since the death of her millionaire husband fourteen years before.

No *wonder* she knew where to pee.

And I read more. I read about Wilson B. Hartley, Ph.D., who was a professor of sociology at Harvard, who was sometimes called Hawk in memory of the jazz saxophonist Coleman Hawkins.

And the other bag ladies? Those phantom people who had appeared that night from behind the trees, as if they'd been waiting for that moment all their lives, and who climbed aboard a swan and sang? They were real. They were real bag ladies — homeless women, the *Herald* called them — and the police let every one of them go. They couldn't fine them because they had no money. They couldn't take them to shelters because there were none. So they turned them all loose that night, back out to the streets, to wander and disappear into the shadows of the scrapheap city once again.

At least they turned them loose with some

memories, I like to think, of that one night in such a sweet, green place.

Looking glumly at the newspaper, at my tangled, messy hair in the photograph, I remembered something: the dumb burglar disguise, the ski cap I had worn that night.

"I lost my best ski hat," I wailed, bursting into tears.

"You can get another one," said Mrs. Kolodny. "That old one never looked too good on you anyway, Enid." She rubbed my back and stroked my hair as a comfort, and I cried and cried.

But my tears weren't really for the crummy old hat. I felt as if I had lost so much else. Mrs. Kolodny massaged my shoulders and back with her gnarled hands, and she murmured, "There now, there now," but she didn't know what I cried for.

It was for lots of things. For Hawk, and the soaring notes that he blew into the night for those lonely ladies, and for all the sociology he taught at Harvard, which could never explain why, as he sat there tall and proud and defenseless, a nightmare voice had yelled: *"Cuff the black guy!"*

I cried for Julia Simpson Forbes, who lived all alone in a penthouse tower and came down to wander each day in a Garden, where most people looked away when she passed because she was old.

And for Seth, because of what he had said before the police dragged him away from me; because I knew he had not said it before and it was not likely he would ever say it again.

But mostly I cried for Tom Terrific. The Hill Heir. Crap. That little kid, with all his funny giggles and bright eyes, had never in his life had a Popsicle, or a bubble bath, or a Swan boat ride, or dirty hands. And now, I knew — because I saw his mother's face when she looked at me in the police station that night — he never would have another chance at any of those things.

It turns out that I won't go to jail after all. Eventually all the charges were dropped. It took a lot of negotiating, my father said, when he was talking to me again.

The last one to let go — she had wanted to charge me with kidnapping — was Ms. Cameron. She was finally talked out of it by my persuasive father, the lawyer; by the police, who were sick of the whole thing; and by Seth's father, the TV magnate. He did a *Heartwarmers* spot about the bag ladies, turning the Swan Boat hijacking into such a heroic tale that probably half of Boston puked watching it. Famous Wilma Sandroff, too, apparently turned on her charm, saying soothing things like, "Your anger is very healthy, Ms. Cameron. I certainly understand your anger."

There were compromises made and prices paid.

We had to pay for the chains we cut, and let me tell you, you'd be amazed at the prices they're getting for chains these days. I contributed all my summer savings, and so did Seth. Hawk wrote a check for his share. Some of Julia Simpson Forbes's millions were kicked in, too, by a man called a conservator who had been appointed to oversee her life. Conservator is just a fancy word for *keeper*, and I cried again when I heard that, that a feisty old lady who can stop all the traffic on Arlington Street with a wave of her hand will now and forever have to ask permission to make a single move.

Seth and I are on an informal sort of probation, which only means we have to go to school and get decent grades and stay out of trouble. We always did that anyway, except for me and geometry. Seth says he'll tutor me in math.

Hawk is on rather bad terms with the Harvard administration because of the embarrassing publicity. But he has tenure, my mother says. I'm not exactly sure what tenure is. If Hawk has it, it's got to be okay. And the police did give his saxophone back.

The worst thing is that I am never to see Tom Terrific again. That was a rule made by Ms. Cameron, and my father said it was absolutely non-negotiable. Ms. Cameron has hired a governess for the Hill Heir. I cringed when I heard that, picturing a hatchet-faced woman in a uniform, slapping his hands and washing his mouth out with soap. Mrs. Kolodny and I know all about governesses from British novels. Mrs. Kolodny says that she grieves and mourns for Tom Terrific, even though she never met him. I grieve and mourn for him, too.

Mrs. Kolodny, sitting in my room with me during that bad time, smuggling me cookies and filling me in on *As the World Turns*, told me to remember that books with sad endings very often have something called an Epilogue. In the Epilogue, it becomes clear that the sad ending was only temporary. "You wait, Enid," said Mrs. Kolodny with her mouth full of oatmeal cookie, "all of this will have an Epilogue for sure."

I do love Mrs. Kolodny. But she is one of the spaciest people I've ever known.

Epilogue

*I*t's a rainy Saturday afternoon in October, and I'm waiting for Seth to come over and help me with the math homework. Mrs. Kolodny is down in the kitchen making brownies because she says that the way to a man's heart is through his stomach. When she said that, while serving pancakes at breakfast, my mother announced that the way to a man's heart is through his superior vena cava, but she was laughing when she said it.

I laughed, too, because I didn't need either one of them to tell me how to find my way into Seth's heart. I seem to have a pretty firm place there already. His interest in tutoring me in math is not really very academic, and we spend a lot of time goofing off and drawing each other's initials in the middle of isosceles triangles. But I didn't say anything at breakfast because it's a good way to get some homemade brownies out of Mrs. Kolodny, although I've got my fingers crossed that she won't burn them on the bottom this time.

A little while ago, the telephone rang. When I answered it, the giggly little voice was so familiar that I almost burst into tears.

"Is your refrigerator running?" he asked.

I bit my lip to keep from crying. "Nope," I said very seriously, "I just ran down the street and caught it."

"Hey!" he sputtered. "You're spozed to say, 'Yes,' and then *I* say —"

"I know that, silly," I said. Then I lowered my voice to a whisper. "How come you're able to call me?"

"My mother's not home," he whispered back.

"But I thought you had a governess now."

"Yeah," he said, and I could almost see his dimpled grin. "I do. She looked up your number for me. But I dialed it all by myself. Guess what we're going to do next!"

"Take a bubble bath?"

"Nope. Eat a pizza. Then we're going to call the mayor, the real mayor of Boston! And we're going to ask him if his refrigerator's running!"

"Tom Terrific," I said, "I love you."

"I love you, too. I gotta go now."

"Okay. Hey. What's her name? Your governess?"

His laughter chimed through the phone. "Promise you won't tell my mother?"

"I promise."

"*Wonder Woman!*"

We kissed each other through the telephone and said good-by.

There was a pad of paper by the phone, and I'd been doodling as I talked to him, drawing little flowers and smiling faces. After I hung up, I printed my name: ENID.

I looked at it for a long time. Then I wrote, under it:

SPLENDID.

SPLENDID.

SPLENDID.

It almost rhymes.